MW01278642

Sporadic Memories

Ali Marsman

ISBN: 978-1-897512-11-1
Copyright © Ali Marsman 2008
All rights reserved
Cover ℞
Saga Books

Sagabooks.net

For the betterment of our world...

It has been so long since the last moment I held you in my arms, and the sweet smell of your sandalwood caressed the motion of my desire.

I always admired
the gracefulness
of your diligence,
the knowledge of
your intelligence,
the caress of your soul,
the height of your intellect
and the warmth from your glow.

I found it so hard to look into your eyes even as the years went by, when our eyes met one another's, we would always send sparks to the groins of one another. Oh baby! I found it so hard looking into your eyes even as the years went by.

It was simply wonderful how the soft moans of our love for one another would soothe the uncertainty of the dreamlike flight we took each other through, in the absolute knowing of ecstasy.

Remembering our first kiss
when we realized the height of our bliss,
we kissed so lightly
French kissed each other slightly
our souls caressed just nicely,

remembering our first kiss always excited the spot
where we first knew we were in love.

There were parallel fireworks that night. The cottage
was done up beautifully; lit candles, flowers all over the
floor, the bed. The fireplace roared, the ocean fierce
against the rocks, the soft circles of our love danced the
fire more, the fierceness of the ocean caused our bodies
to pour, and there were parallel fireworks that night.

We always accepted the knowledge of what our souls
have acquired through the days, arose each other to a
place where others longed to be, which opened our
spirit to a feeling never embodied before, caused our
wings to be exposed, caused our hearts to soar, how we
desired more! We always accepted each other, which
caused our greatness to show.

I have incredible memories of our dates, and how we
would bring presents to one another, like candles and
sweet grass. It was a perfect summer's evening. We
arrived at the beach just as the colors in the sky were
changing, setting the mood peacefully. We had a picnic
as we watched the sunset, and the stars emerged to light
our mood delightful. We confessed how we were both
very much in love, you gave me one of two bracelets
you had made, and we placed them on the opposite
wrists of one another. Hands connected, bracelets
touching, we both knew in the same instant we found
what we desired for so long, and from that moment
onward . . . we always had our bracelets brushing.

We accepted one another as our hearts so desired
admired the hesitation

of our chills, and fires
opened ourselves up completely
not at all afraid
we were acutely impassioned
in awe for our days.

Memories of you come up sporadically throughout
the days, not having one another, holding one another,
helping one another feel at ease. I dream so often of us
lying in bed whispering the details of our growth of
love, combined with strokes of passion on each other.
I dream so often
the comfort of your
entirety,
the ways in which
you revealed you to me,
how every ounce of pain
was healed spiritually,
the gracefulness
of our passages
involved each other's energies,
our body, mind, and spirit
interlocked wonderfully,
simply appropriated to each other
faithfully.

Now not in a moment, with a simple gaze into each
other's eyes, rather, it was a courtship that stimulated
over time, like the harmony that is inspired in an
established bottle of wine.

We treated one another with sensitivity,
showered one another with sweet details of speech,
excited and eager to learn, to teach,

gave comfort through simplicity in our laughter
and the obliviousness of time,
I could rely on your exuberance
as you were confident in mine,
our eyes so deep
therefore we both could see,
the deepness that lay
within our eternity,
the wind caught our breath
as we roamed the ground
barefoot and exposed,
hands placed on the heart
pressing firmly on the chest,
helping each other rest,
soothing the tenderness
of the day's long journey,
assuring our love
through this path,
provoking one's most passionate desires
removing one's biggest fears
embracing one another
love that is absolute
holding our bodies as one,
assuring our love
spirits willing,
assuring our love
it has been so long since the last moment.

It has been so long since I tasted the sweetness of your
hot apple cider as we sat comfortably in front of the fire
in a blanket I made for us. I go back often to the days we
would massage the weekends away, taking care in
appeasing one another while dripping in crystalline
sparkle, unaware of the day. With the rotation of

mending in our palms we would release the wounds,
and celebrate through song; I can still feel the palms of
you, now freeing the throes of our journey without you.

Under the apple tree we planted many years ago, the
heat of our creativity flourished its growth. We painted
one another under its shield, with the background, the
flowers of our field. With the healing power of nature as
its trim, we embrace the seductiveness in the Jasmine.
We pick them carefully; place them in a heart around,
the outline for our creative ground. My body the center
is exposed, you create the passionate side of our fate,
your body exposed and I am inspired, creating your
fiery heart I desire. Fires, fires, burning fires, we always
kept the fires burning, with moans, and groans, and
subtle tones; the fires always burned in and around our
home.

We would hang our paintings on the wall of our
bedroom to be reminded of the passion inspired 'Under
the Apple Tree' title one, title two 'Our Burning Desire'
As the days rolled by love continued to unfold, with
swift movements, and the charming demonstration of
what lay in advance, showing off for one another at
every chance, submissiveness, and influence with
captivating dance. Music soft, our love is close as we
move together, feeling the beats of our hearts, the
firmness of our embrace, the dancing of our groins,
breathing together, soft music; we always enjoyed the
evenings after 'Our Burning Desire Under the Apple
Tree'

I have been so sad since I lost you my tears I cannot
suppress, the warmth of you at night is gone, and

therefore, I cannot rest. The pacification I felt as you
untroubled me against you . . . I miss
head on your shoulder
hand on your back
head on my pillow
hand rubbing my back
whispering love before sleep
so pleasant dreams we would keep
awakening every single morning feeling aglow
with a rise of knowing in our souls.
I have been lost without the love I received from the tips
of your fingers running across my body excitedly. You
knew my body well. Circles around my neck, shiver
aloud, gliding down my spine, rise up, shivers aloud,
and moan,
loving me so easily
kissing always passionately
pleased consistently with generosity
making love a specialty
with your strong sense of being
you exemplified true meaning
softly...slowly, always soft, and slow
gently caressed me
gradually undressed me
thoroughly explored me
my mind always ecstasy
swell and burst
over and over...
my mind tasting ecstasy
while exploring your body
held you oh
so close to me
kissed you softly and slowly
peaking with synchronicity.

Shoulders influenced by passion in hammers striking strings, you lured me closer each time with the harmony you would bring. The keys played so beautifully, my, you played well! When the piano you would sound, my heart swelled. I loved to hear the music softly, I loved hearing it boom; notes chasing one another in every single room. Your voice; the ways you would sing to me, I miss you dedicating me songs...

`To show my love for you
to thank you for all you do,
for lifting my spirits high
to prove how much you mean to me
for the entire world to see,
I would write a message through the sky
for the entire world to see
just what you mean to me,
to show happiness you bring
this is the song I sing'

I long for one more Sunday under the waterfall with bare feet, drumming and moving to the beats of hands blending on skin. Our hearts opened with every boom, chanted for our love that which opened up our higher heart, and accessed unconditional love... 'AH, AH, AH, AH, AH, AH, AH' over and over and over and over; touching the feel of one another, leaning against one another, love like a blanket we enjoyed it like that! Kept us with warmth, security in the dark; kept warm in love in darkness under the waterfall, illuminated only by the glow of the sweet grass, the sparkle from the sun. Drumming, chanting to the beats of the drum on Sunday.

It is symbiotic; rather it must have been; fate, we were a valuable connection from the beginning. Our energies collided, our souls embraced, giving us the same in love feelings of the heart. We lived for the moment, every occasion spent to grow; we embraced the dedication in nurturing each soul. All love mutual, flowed naturally, together in love, you and me. Today is Sunday, and you drum with me in spirit, and your chants still blend with mine under the waterfall.

My heart was lonely as I roamed the grounds of where the exhibition was held so long ago. I sat at the spot where the merry-go-round was, that was our favorite ride. I closed my eyes and could feel the closeness of your chest pressing cozy against my back, arms around me, hands fastened, delicately moving to the music playing and whispering love. As I sat, I could taste the sweetness of the candy apples we enjoyed as we listened to the excitement and laughter in those around us. Including their energies into ours, willing our high spirits even closer and leaving on an animated rise. As I left the grounds of where the exhibition was held, I placed a Sweet William plant from our garden there, so that the close clusters of the sweet-smelling flowers it blossoms, will forever exude the coziness of the ride on the merry-go-round, and the sweetness of the candied apples mixed with laughter in the breeze.

You are needed in the mornings just before the sun is rising, breathing in the freshness of the new day together, and stretching to the sounds of baby birds eager for their meal. A celebration, rejoicing our unity, started every day off including nature feeling enlarged!

Breakfast does not seem that important to me any more since you have been gone. The preparation no longer illustrates our journey together. I sit alone and become saddened by memories of how much time we took to enjoy our morning meal; choosing which flowers would be placed at the center of the table, watching me watch you. A flower that symbolized our beauty, one that personified our spirit, and one for rapture, watching you watch me, choosing oh, so carefully. My flowers in the vase are lonely without yours leaning against them; uniting them, welcoming their energies with ours . . . it is sometimes too difficult to pick the nature of our morning meals without you.

We moved through life together in triple time, to the throbbing of our liveliness, the excitement of our path. We talked of life and ways to develop spiritually on our soul joining expedition. The ways in which we included others, leaving long-lasting impressions while receiving them, continuously embed flashes in my view. I always think about you. You came up over tea past evenings, how content you were while sustaining yourself, as I maintained me, writing of life and how I feel about thee, while you painted and sipped on tea. The inspiration has ended, I can only write of all I remember of you, the flashes I see of you and the burning in my hips for you. Dance! You would dance for me exotically, enticed me effectively, danced close to me…exuded your energy positively. I miss you. I get sad about every day from thinking about you, and all night dreaming about you.

We weighed in each other's with, lit up one another's lives, held our meaning of life together at the highest of value, appreciated life, and what we were destined to do; I never imagined I would be this lost without you, so many times I do not know what to do, everything reminds me of you. I traveled about on our field last afternoon while the sun was splendid, sat down and started to collect thoughts of sadness over you, the brilliance of the sun got me through, while I grieved for you.

I enjoy remembering the smiles of you, how they caused my eyes to shine, and contented me further in the absolute knowing of ecstasy. I long for our united spirituality, the solace of our sexuality, our corresponding solacing unity and spiritual sexuality. I am so sad thinking about all the wonderful times we had, I write alone with my pen dealing with my loss over you, at no time will I ever grow tired of my memoirs of you, just overwhelmed with tearfulness over the loss of you, getting through on thoughts of happy times spent with you.

There was always laughter in the snow, and excitement in the rain; we thrived from the richness of the moisture, and the motion of the breeze, the richness of the moisture in the breeze. Traveling about in an ambling way and caused the shadows of others to sway with ours in the breeze. Marking declarations; depositing beneficial points of embodying our inherent spirituality. Excitement in the rain; holding hands, splashing in the puddles, coming home muddy then showering one another in a flow of tangerine therapy, feeling revitalized, refreshed and energized. Hot chocolate in front of the fire revealing smiles of our experiences in the rain, how I long for that once again, all the fun we had in the rain.

We basked in the enlightened feeling during therapy
of green tea, inspired insightful tones of creativity,
working as you motivated me, and illustrated me, while
enjoying the joyful, uplifting feeling we found from the
ginger lily, in the surroundings of our domain, plunged,
and consuming nature's therapy.

Our setting was of high treasure, for the blanket of its
security, to the vastness of its view, the lushness of its
scene...forever, just as our love! Relaxing on a field of
wild flowers; the blue columbine reminded us of the
stars at night, as we imagined the sounds of the
bluebells. The climbing fragrance of the twining
honeysuckle blended with the sun-like characteristics of
the dandelions...painted the image of our demesne as I
wrote quietly with ease, so close to the apple tree, while
in a pool of green tea therapy.

Exploring the plains of a wondrous land; riding
through shafts of grass that reach past the top of our
wheels; surrounded by the Acacia, and fierce call of the
wild. Destination, to the heart of the jungle! Being drawn
to the sounds of drums, shakers, and tambourines...A
Celebration! Cleansing their bodies of the impurities,
welcoming us into their circle, teaching a song to replay
in our soul, said it would help our spirit grow, enhance
us even further, help undercover things not yet known.
The moaning of our love grew deeper as we explored
warmth on that mighty terrain, how I long for that
feeling again, forever will remain our growth of love on
the terrain.

It was our anniversary, sundown; we rejoiced in the

lifelong endeavor of the soul's tenderness, joined with another at its best, yours and mine put to the test. Made merry of our faithfulness on a joining sure to remain, dancing on the mighty terrain to the sounds of drums, tambourines and shakers...shaking...shook us closer to the height of our bliss...kiss, passion, shaking on the terrain.

You loved me; we loved each other together in a prideful way, displayed liberal communications, and discarded an unfamiliar ness, of superficial blissfulness. Surrounded only by others who were developing their path, taught their knowledge. Our friends sure do miss you, we visit frequently, we speak of you and enjoy the rest of our journey together, uniting our spirits with the changes in the weather, and continuing to spend anniversaries together. After all these years still toasting to the belief that 'One hundred percent of positive ness, will raise us to the point of successfulness, in reaching our level of a human kindness' It gets me through, being surrounded by all who love you, love me, love them, we toast in your memory 'Here, Here!'

The peacefulness at dinnertime is with me even now, sitting at the table; I can see the shadow of you sitting in the chair. Candles are burning, still feels like you are here, telling me how much you care, while consuming our meal, we made such a big deal. I can taste the sharp light of our flame for one another; the burning still remains. The sharpness of the meal coating my body's wholesome need, keeping me lively on our path, those feelings linger with me now as I sit and recall the heat that engulfed me.

Uttering my name never quite the same way, dependent on the nature of the feeling, but always passionate in your pronunciations, understood by my listening and hearing. Calling me out over the breeze, 'return to me please' followed the patterns in the breeze, which led me back to thee. Calling you out in my sleep because of the life-life dreams I would keep, turning yours with mine, calling out in oblivious time. Arousing the heart of one another to get the centers of us dancing, dancing to the patterns in our dreams, begging you to come with me please, defining a dripping reverie. We would seldom awake. We participated in all aspects of our fate, helped us sleep deeper with one another; we came with the utterances of names.

It was three o'clock in the morning when I was awakened from my dream. My heart was pounding, by body wet; it was inordinate desire for thee. Three o'clock in the morning, and I am awakening alone, crying out for you 'come back to me please, why did you have to leave on our spirit's journey, the purpose was for you and me, combining the knowledge of what we learned and believe, you were not supposed to leave so early' That happens sometimes, after all these years I continue to awake to the illusion that you have not left me, means that you are here with me, even if not all physically. You bring me back merrily to grasping solidarity at an important level greater than before, with me to guide, because in spirit you remain.

The photographs are taking me back to the times you performed. I have pulled them out tonight with the thunderstorm. Sitting at the piano baby and grand, beautifully enunciating your fingers with the keys, raising the shivers in those around you, but especially in me. Oh how you seduced my mind with the rhyming of your fingers, stimulating as you performed, singing about the struggles on lands. They were always benefit performances to make changes in the world, sang about peace and joy. Raised funds for medicine and food, performed with others to help grow, and expressed the need for support through your music, superior in its cause. Through your music we caught the theme, filled our souls each time we completed a means. The pictures sure do take me back to your greatness, oh how your integrity glows, devotion shown, in the images of you performing.

I am celebrating your birthday today, taking me back to the suspense of surprises for the day I prepared ahead of time carefully without your knowledge. The measured quality in the selection of music playing brought us to our desired mood, while I fixed dinner, an occasion I prepare alone for this day...

Two teaspoons finely snipped fresh thyme
one teaspoon finely snipped fresh rosemary
two teaspoons dried juniper berries, crushed
cup dry Vermouth
cup apple jelly (homemade)
Salmon fillets
freshly ground black pepper
extra rosemary and thyme to garnish
homemade bread

Toasting the juniper until fragrance, boiling the Vermouth to toast the berries, adding much of the rosemary and thyme, simmer in the apple jelly, heat one minute then set aside. Preheat oven 400 degrees while in a skillet brown salmon backside up first then front then add to an ovenproof pan. Spoon glaze carefully over each fillet, sprinkle garnish smoothly over each fillet...bake. Serve with rice, fresh vegetables, homemade bread, candles, a large bouquet and champagne.

Dinner was after the picnic on the island. It was an extraordinary voyage over the ocean, the clearness of the sky exaggerated the suns burning, reflecting our heart's yearning. The richness of the moisture in the breeze, birds flying with the motion of the breeze, as we enjoyed wine, and all its subtleties.

We chose the highest point on the island and sat down to consume the contents of the basket, the chocolate dipped fruit being our favorite.
'Happy birthday honey
I hope you are having a wonderful time
I toast to you a glass of wine
My arms for you are opened wide
in this poem
there is a hug inside
I have also sealed it with a kiss
a passionate one
to express our bliss
Happy birthday honey'

We left the island on a height that provoked our composure, enjoying the gentle ride back over the ocean, while anxious to return, left the island while our hips still burned.
The fireworks happened after dinner. It was already

sundown when I lured you down to the lake through a
path I started working on the morning after your last
birthday...this is the first time you have seen it!

Green grass with shafts that stay so perfect even after
being walked upon, rows of red, yellow, pink, and white
carnations, lilies, tulips, and sunflowers, all beautifully
placed in rows wide enough to run through...selecting a
few. Arriving at the gazebo, you sit as I place the flowers
all around, blanketing the entire ground. Holding you,
while toasting to you, the burning in our hips we could
not bear anymore, I laid you gently down on the
flowered floor, the fireworks happened as they have
before, the calmness in the lake helped our bodies to
pour. Moved slowly to the serenity of the breeze, juices
saturating the petals and the leaves, come, come, come
back to me please.

It has been a long time since we walked together at
night, guided by the moon and low beam of the fireflies
in search of a spot clear enough to see perfectly the stars.
We would often travel through the soft and hard woods
that appeared connected at the top, impeding our view
of the light, causing us to hold one another closer as we
journey in search of our destination. It was not a very
long walk; it seldom was with us before the trees opened
up appearing the distance in our view. We gathered
leaves, and placed them in piles comfortable enough to
rest, took off our shoes to massage the feet of our rugged
means of separateness, at a spot which revealed a bright
darkness in the sky. We sat with our back securely
supporting one another, gazing at opposite poles upon
the depth of the atmosphere, head on your shoulder,
arms interlocked with mine, connecting the points of our

energies with constellation lines.

Back through the path of ruggedness we return home to our sanctum bliss, and recount feelings found in the deepest of upper limits, by the light of the moon penetrating through the windows in our ceiling. This room was pleasant, still is, I frequent it often to recall times shared with you after our journeys, my journeys alone. We named it Sanctum Ness, our creation for holiness, visited on Sundays after drumming, and chanting under the waterfall. Invocations for our profits to 'please guide us delicately on our spirit's destiny, help us welcome the knowledge of this combined security, and open us up completely spiritually'

Beseeching your air once and anew, my eyes I dry in this room without you, looking through the windows at the spectacular view, time, too much time has gone by without you.

You were amazed at my direction in writing plays, said I captivated audiences in mysterious ways, and moved the crowd as you did as the keys you played. My performances were of the same benefit as yours; through my words I expressed the need for social support. Acting of what was seen on similar lands, expressing through action, while you performed with your hands, the need for support on lands.
This is where our souls united. Fate were to have it, we were both performing that night, we could feel the passionate side of our young glow, could feel the dedication illuminating from each old soul, realized before our hearts could know, performing in that show was inevitable.

Too much time has passed since we sat at the window's bay together; the inspiration from its view gave us gentleness while writing dialogue and music to be used. It was not too long before we brought our work together, knew we just had to bring us together, play music and act together through that level of human kindness, the kindness of humans expressed in a creative way, through the motion of your fingers, joined together with my plays.

Act one, scene two

Serwa, an African woman is seated with her legs parted, and straight. As she gazes with tearful eyes at the audience in the seats above, the spotlight reflects her. Piano sound lightly...Serwa begins.

Each day I walk through rugged and dangerous terrain in search of water clear, and plentiful enough to sustain my family for another day. My husband and I had seven children, two have left us, they were sick. My husband has left us too, he was too sick. I am dying. I do not have medicine, my immunities are diminishing quickly, I rely on the rituals of the villages' spiritual people, my spiritual keeper. My name is Serwa, and I get sick, but I still must walk those miles in search of water.

Spotlight fades from Serwa, at the same time it is focusing on the top left of the stage where Chunna, an Asian woman, is squatting, looking at the floor in despair, piano sound lightly playing.

I am all alone. My family left me on the streets when I

was a little girl, why? Because I was no longer pure, they said it was my fault. After a while I was taken in, I was forced to perform in dance shows to feed myself, to have a little bit of money; I performed backstage for extra money. They always took my babies before they were ready. I am sick. I am no longer taken in; I do not have money to keep my body well. Dying . . . alone once again on the streets with no one to count on.

Spotlight fades from Chunna while focusing on a Pakistan woman kneeling on the floor, piano lightly playing.

I am Kimeri, though it means nothing here. You cannot see my face, only my eyes, which reveal my pain, it does not matter though. I am forbidden to speak, I am always afraid, my body does not belong to me, a piece of me is lost every day, all night. I am sick, but I do not matter, I sit frightened on the streets dying alone with my battles . . .

Spotlight appears on all three women, same line . . .
But it doesn't matter here when you are woman.
I am woman.
Hear power in my name.
Serwa; noblewoman.
My name means the same.
Kimeri, a woman.
Hear struggles in my name.
(Chunna)
Why is it that everywhere
we are treated the same?
what does it matter
all the power,

and struggles of our name
(all)
when all over the world
we are treated the same?

The celebrations were incredible after the show,
people surrounding us, and telling us how our great
nature truly shows. The smiles and warm hugs are with
me as I withdraw, the reasons we were brought
together, and the ways in which we answered our call.

We took many vacations together to places filled with
knowledge about the spirit, learned so much about how
to take care of ourselves, while taking carefulness
around. Visited many grounds to enhance our way, not
only developing ourselves, but also replacing growth
along the way. Improving all of our knowledge,
bartering in a way, sitting in circles around the world,
feeding each other the simple pleasures, ours with
theirs, theirs with ours. Bringing forth our celebrations
together, drumming, chanting, calling out for each other,
taking firm hold of the hands of one another, thriving
from energies forming a whole, a feeling that naturally
matured our souls, as we participated with the world.

Cheerless without you, lately my heart stumbles with
the loss of you, my soul does not know what to do, the
writings on my paper are sadness over you . . . giving
myself up without you. I need guidance through this
consuming despondency that is with me, somewhat
stays within me. Memories lifts in my soul, please, help
my faithful character show, glow, slowly back to me.

You sang to me in my sleep last night, held me closely

through the night 'hush my little angel; now do not cry
for me. I have not left you for a moment on our soul's
destiny. Feel my energy next to yours caressing the
painfulness against the tenderness, believe our unity;
keep faith that it remains unchanged. Let me continue to
be motivation for thee, through unpredictable memories,
mirage, and prepared ones of me. Close your eyes, and
forever count on me, our love will not recede, leave,
there are too many great memories'

The reliance of our path bounces again in my soul;
brought my liveliness down to a controllable means
without you, with you in a mystical way, through the
rest of my days, keeping me together on my path,
together on our path.

You know our love still feels as if it is growing, has
grown. I can hear the subtle tones of your heart
moaning, toning mine to yours through memories, a
selection of thoughts gathered up on you, all this writing
gets me through. Expressed with many words,
inescapable sounds, and gestures as I write, observing
everything we used to do. It fosters my sharing on this
path, sureness in me to help this last, 'The Kindness of
Human's Path'
I continue to work for what we were brought here to
do, and all over the world people honor you, credit me,
regard us.

'For the changes you brought together
to our land,
for the warmth of your embraces, and
the heat from your hands,
for helping our land grow

to impress our souls,
for soothing the idea
that there was nowhere to go;
you helped pave the way
forever your spirits will remain
over our land to stay,
you brought forth together
fuller days
for this,
we honor you together'

   That was one of the celebrations we were invited to,
we were honored in, helps me to continue our cause, the
tokens of appreciation, the respect, and applause. This
all brings me back to the importance of lending my
creativity; to help others pass survival while I carry on
through, guiding and growing with others within the
spirit of you. You linger with me; I can hear your fingers
at the keys as I sit at the bay, gathering sounds and
visions to replay.

We were happy as our bracelets brushed as we walked
along the beach. Took pleasure in the sand covering our
feet as the waves splashed up to clean them, a pattern
we made a game of, while enjoying the sun, the
laughter, the fun in us, all of us. Remembering running
from the waves, jumping over them, sitting with our
backs to them, as their strength massaged us. Oh the
pleasures healing us as we fulfilled us, staying to watch
the sun go down, the radiant colors of the sky matched
the quality of our hue, the red easily agreed with the red
in your cheeks for me, in mine for you. The burning
quality in the colors changed consistently, disappeared
quickly as we watched the stars appear, holding one

another, gazing at the furthest star...closing our eyes hoping 'for our love to last reciprocated, keep us playful on our path each day it is dated, from the moment we were brought together, keep the excitement the same, keep an equal amount of ambition while calling each other's name, keep our love the same' as we smiled and held one another on the beach.

I long for one more celebration of my birthday with you, it was cozy. Remembering you bathing with me in a pool of mixed rose petals, massaging my body, our shadows passionate on the walls. My echoes a reflection of you obeying me, calling out for you . . . please! Danced my shadow on the wall, melted me as I performed in the show, wanting, and not letting go as we celebrated in a pool of rose petals.

Riding horse-drawn carriage through the trail in the snow around the lake in the evening as the light crackle from the bamboo torches loosened us, relaxed us, warmed us. You placed as many as my years, could feel the growth of heat as you placed them nearer to one another, riding, and holding each other, listening to a song on the tape recorder you brought along, you wrote for me, 'Merry of Your Start' that song replays in my heart each year I celebrate without you, horse-drawn carriage around the lake.

I have a craving for your hot apple pie; I just cannot make it the way you did, with the combination of spices as immaculately as you did. The outer layer fluffy, and baked to beautify the contents it held, intensifying the shell through its contents, mouth-watering unfailingly, on my special occasion you presented to me, a slice of your specialty, with a candle in the middle. It is too difficult to try to eat the apple pie, for I cannot bear that yearly ache in my belly for thee.

Rowing to the soft ripples on the lake, tossing petals, and flowers we brought along from our field, leaning close to one another whispering 'love me, love me more, and more, love me' Calling out over the lake, 'I, I, Love, Love, You, You' throwing petals in the lake merrily back, 'I Love You, I Love You' Tossing petals in the sky, as you echo my name, as beautifully as the days, I gently called your name, 'you mean so much to me, I never imagined this amount of congruency existed, constant bliss, oh how this love I miss' as I gently toss petals, and write about thee.

Surrounded by a love created rainbow flower, our canoe bopped rhythmically upon the waves as we rested ourselves to the slight current in the wind, the course of the birds, and the direction of our love. We gazed on one another, and talked of the contented chills of our fires, while riding the wave of our existence. The passion and feelings are with me today as I retrace our path, relaxing on the lake, enjoying the solitude, and the opportunity to recall memories of you, the smile of you sitting across from me musically in the boat.

We were working together for quite awhile when our passion became obvious. We just finished up one of our shows, and we decided to venture off in search of a place where we could be alone. It was raining just a little that night, the stars were shadows through the mist as we drove this incredible route with trees alongside us that went on forever, but with breaks every so often of inlets. We did not say but a few words; rather we glanced at each other, a reminder of how fantastic we felt, driving and listening to the silence of us. Requiring no discussion on the events soon to unfold, the reassurance of our smiles was enough to guide our souls. We drove for a while when we noticed a vacancy sign off the side of the road, we pulled in. They only had one room available, and we took it, only one bed, a single, and we slept adjoining each other all night, wondering why so long this desire we fought. From the beginning we knew we held the same value for life, and we were brought together for one reason, well that night we were sure, and we held each other touching from that moment forward.

We awoke that morning feeling . . . I doubt we ever found a word suitable enough to express how we felt, we just knew that we matched perfectly for each other, and looked forward to spending time together now that we were for sure.

I hold the collection of photographs you gave me on no particular occasion, at arm's reach of me. I pick them up and imagine the motions all depicting the similar ness of our pose in closeness, and of shows. Capturing us with the same amount of dedication pronounced upon our being, true-to-life memories with the album you filled with images of our beginning, entitled, 'Absolutely You and I'

They follow the increase of our production, shadowing with the expansion of lust, the gradual joining of knowing and trust, our energy and similar way if being captured on film; I keep at arm's length, to pick up the background essence of our being.

While sitting amongst the flowers on a hill a sudden sun shower dampens us, so fresh was the air. A color arch appeared in the sky; we held hands and ran together toward the reflection of the refraction of the sun, mixing in order to the falling rain. Our eyes focused on the top of the rainbow that is where we imagined ourselves to be, sliding down opposite sides to flip the arch around, as bright as it was it still seemed sad. We eagerly reached the top, sat with our backs pressing for a moment. One, two, three go! Screaming with our arms in the air, we quickly slid down, turned the rainbow right side around and reveled in the imagination between you and me.

We had an appetite for the creation of ultimate desired places, awakened by strong emotions written, and illustrious delivery at the keys, motivating me, dancing the ambiance, as I write to the aura of your fingers teasing me, deciding which keys to play, as I write about how I want to kiss you please! Softly, so slowly at the keys, our lips met with harmony, breathing through the music, through descriptions on the page, every time we looked at one another, the tempo began a change.

Imagination wild upon the pages, play my fibers, let your fingers challenge the rhythm of my step, my shoulders moving my back as you intensify the keys, stirring your thoughts with mine, studied specifically, creating love written with beautiful music embracing me. Raised the levels of our desires through strokes fantasized on my page, expressed through your musical wave, our shoulders together sway as we enrapture one

another, through our expression we captured each other,
lured one another with the music of the written word,
the writing of the word, smoothly I seduce my way over
to you.

   I fall apart each time I recall the seduction of me with
the reverence of you, the aftermath correctly represents
the details of our musical play, played and written on
looks, and acted upon a private stage.
Seductive with deep eyes
following slowly
intense sighs
hands join in
stimulating skin
words a whisper
as we begin
inspired desires
awaiting fires
our love, higher
as we calm the
overwhelming ness
of throbbing chills
sobbing chills
as we switch scenes
elevate further into
the end
we end together . . . suddenly the show is over, but we
have not let go of the feeling. We lay together dripping,
bringing ourselves peacefully to sleep, knowing; subtle
strokes of appreciation will be delivered through the
night, and accepted through grinding, and groaning,
and fluidity of our dream, one image of our ecstasy.

   Creatively my hand prepared evenly the particulars of

your features as you lay on the hearth. While studying the combination of the smoothness of your mixture path, thoughts stir in me. Steadily I begin the stroke, moving in delicate circles around the page . . . mmm you look so radiant tonight, captured faultlessly by the crackling light, relaxed precisely to the time of night, the crackling light. The easiness in the selection playing gave us gentle tones, moans, and subtle groans, gratifying one another through inspiration, motivation, motivating me, grinding and moaning just a little for me, while holding your pose for me, as I stroke so delicately.

The inspiration is complete and I sign my name to thee, on the lighted crackling scene, entitled it 'you and me' You slowly moved over and took the brush from me, brushed tiny circles stimulating me, moving your body next to me, shivers, shivering, jerking with me, sporadically, pressingly.

Photographed me. To combine the work of your imagination on top of mine, included on me, on the center of you. Our mixtures blending about the site, exactly experiencing the center light of the hearth, picture, placed securely on your heart. Glowing, still moaning we made our way over to the bed, letting go, embracing the feeling of out of control ness, the boundless bliss of this partnership. Coming with one another to the point of an uncontrollable means, controlling the means, brought to life the scene of you and me.

As I watch the scene fall into a colorless phase, I find myself bringing back memories of us, how we brought to life the dreariness of its view. Our easy voices made

for exact hearing in our wants of one another, guided
brightness in each other, and upheld interest in each
other. Desires blowing through the wind, it is so easy to
see the sky during this time, the sun still warm through
the cold air, guided our way as we included our energies
with the changing days. Something was just so magical
in the air during this season, an inspirational presage
that got us in the mood, an overpowering creativeness
which could not be eluded; establishing visions after the
scene has fallen...

Reading me; sitting comfy in the blanket summarizing
me, the story of one who wrote of fantastic journeys
taken over the vastest of seas, the mightiest of rains, the
excitement for fantasy engaged, intensified by
descriptions of the oceans easy rage. Writing away,
being taken away, being blown by the wind with an
enthusiastic finish of each page . . .

Chapter One: The Peaceful Isle

Not complete solitude, I mean the perfection of this island from the sun, and its proximity to the stars, gives you that feeling of completeness in being alone with yourself, helps you feel at ease with patterns that may provoke negative emotions on one's self. You actually feel as if you can reach the stars, your wishes are that much closer, so many of them fall; it is like fireworks on clear nights. Falling asleep while listening to the sounds of the birds bringing peace and relaxation through the silence of the resting nights. The waves deliver sounds of passion; can't write about the passion on the island all alone with oneself, so the waves deliver guidance, points which way the wind is blowing, preparation for when the voyage should commence again...

Accepting my words as they pour out of me, through notes of acknowledgment, and agreement with the expressions. As smooth as my language you flow your rhythm, tiny shivers showing on skin, the tiniest details of my speech harmonizing with your fingers as you play so eloquently, my words flow effortlessly to your music...with mine. A slow ballad, your music matching mine, played calmly in G, my words a lower key, play, play me! Hear together the keys, my words writing your song, your music writing my words.

Come closer
soft hands
you know just where to touch me
mmm...
I know where when it is my time
kiss me

mmm...
soft lips
hesitation at the keys
music drifting off
in a calmly played glee
showing all over you and me
hold me closer please
reach around me to the keys
to the beat we are moving, play!
harmony with the keys
sustaining you and me
fingering delicately...the keys
ending abruptly!

In the darkness it breaks my heart caressing the place where you once slept, where mutual dreams were kept, now alone. Oh how sad it is to be without you, now the dreams have changed, a continuation of my solitary days, turning yours no more. I am bothered by the weakness felt in the center of me, and of my groins, rising on their own to you, missing you, wanting to grind yours once again. This is the beginning of the end living life without you. I will cry tomorrow of the smiles now past, not forgotten, ones you often gave to me under the hue of the tree we planted.

Many years ago I recall this very spot, feels like the exact time of day, the same type of day. The similar ness in the way the air is moving brings me back to the day, we remained outside from early morning, to the sun rising the next day. Had picnics all day long, no particular occasion, simply celebrating the flow of our day, days past, and days to come, basking excitedly in all day sun. Shine lighting us as we recall stories of our days, some stories turned us on, so we would bask in our tones together, nice ones just like mine, losing time, kissing your smile. Never again will I kiss your smile, nor will I pull the energy of your laugh with mine, or caress the smoothness of our souls' determined spirit, with the spirit of our souls' combined.

It has been so long since your skin brushed up against me...lying naked in bed, our smiles often turned into laughter, soft, sudden, sporadic sparks of delighted elation. The energy of mine combined with thine, dancing time, losing time, coming to...still kissing your smile. Smiling with me about you and me, energized energy awakening between you and me, I am so sad dreaming about our souls' spirit intensity, it was about you and me.

Insomnia has captured me again tonight, keeping me from the dreamy state that which prepares me of the next day's fill. Capturing inspired insights through the silence of the resting nights, the luminous points illuminating moonlight shown through peacefulness of inspiration as I write of our tones: Our tones were always subtle in both rhythm and in time, consistently on time, interlocked at the same time. All the time we kept our motions moving through the nights, whispering together our dreams insight, that which rested our beings, and inspired our souls. Through the movement of our tones, my timing now less vibrant, my timing now alone, for it is without the deepness of your moans, your light tones just like mine. Missing time without thee, sleeplessness capturing me differently, wanting you with me.

I am lonely quite heavily as I sit and watch alone the changes in the sky at night now that the new season is nearer. Each evening the stars are that much clearer as I gaze upon their brightness on my own listening to the silence everywhere, flowing peacefully throughout the air. I am not too sure why, but it just is, blending precisely to the way I am, as dark as the sky with brightness shining through, as calm as the wind with gusts of sadness blowing in the loss of you. The meaning has changed. Eleven nights awake thinking of the times we shared living awake in life's meaning; now I am left dreaming sleeplessness amongst the darkness over you, I am so sad you see, I just want it back you know, 'you and me'

Resting my mind tonight, enjoying one of those meditating nights with the glow from the fireplace. Clearing all thoughts from my mind, piercing relaxation, deep breathing, so still, soothing my mind with its soft scent; fragrant frankincense one of our favorite incense savoring throughout the room as I drift further into inner smoothness. Relaxing time passing by, easing my mind through breaths concentrated, no sadness of you in between them, just for now my mind rests.

The words of the picture are so very clear to me, capturing my smile exactly as it was the day it was taken, each time I pass it by, your words speak to me. Placed softly upon my face, a smile; remembering the words of your creation posing my expressions naturally. You did not have to say much for me to give lighting to the pose, just from looking at thee I would glow, my eyes would automatically shine, my head tilted just right, smiling subtly and bright. Had me blending with the scene, the background set off seemingly the essence of me, all captured in a photo that invigorates me each time I pass it by.

The love for you still remains in the place where love is held, right in the center of me, it continues to move throughout my body, and this is why I continue to bleed. These memories are reminding me of just how much we loved, and what it means to have it stopped, not forgotten, but sometimes misplaced. I need you mostly during the nights under the incandescent lights, which shines quietly at night, where all of you was bright, which filled us delightfully. We talked on love before the flames burning, moved the flames as we massaged one another, and spoke before the light; I cannot seem to rest without that. Yes I was left with great memories of thee! This is why recollections are saddening me...it is so different loving living alone. I need you after the night has gone, and the sun begins to shine, I want to prepare with you breakfast once again, stroll amongst the flowers, select a few of them anew. These memories are teasing me, and at the same time pleasing me, expressing the happiness with sadness for thee.

The sensations of our sounds will not be removed from my body, will not escape my mind, nor be forgotten in spirit. The sensations called out for me as they were moving you, tingling our bodies, like little bumblebees we felt the sensations of our sounds moving. Moving to the sounds like music playing, mesmerized by your lips moving, my lips doing for you. Sounds thrilling you, chills willing you further with me, flavors filling the scene; knowledge carnal, total ecstasy of you and me.

Every now and again I can taste the sweet flavors of
your skin on my lips, which rises a little the hips of me,
while pleasing shudders follow the tiny release from me.
You still cause me to moan at unexpected times
throughout the day, I find myself suddenly perplexed
by what it was that I felt. Seemingly tapping into me,
touching memories on me, especially as I sleep, because
of the involuntary feelings I am having; dreaming
exactly of you, generating a physical closeness with you
in peace. It is getting me through, all these thoughts
being released through the tip of my pen, I return feeling
from thee.

You came upon me in my dream last night flowed
smoothly your love over me, uttered your thoughts to
me, fingers tickling me, excitement from the highest
level in us in my dream. Letting go easily because there
was always trust, a must reciprocation naturally, made
real the lust, as if our first time together we touched. In
my dream last night the sounds at times too much,
crystalline sparkle juices lush, paralyzed us as we made
slow the rush of the feelings, sounds effused, and
gushed. Secure sensations trusted one another as you
came upon me in my sleep, real images I keep the same
in me, moves the deepness of me, as I make real earlier
days.

As you lay asleep most nights my hands would caress
your entirety, drifting further into deepness you would
go with assurance from me. I would often stay awake
past thee, writing in bed next to you inspiring me. My
hip fitting nicely along your side, as my calf caresses

your thigh, you were really good at resting through those pen scratches, and body strokes of mine. Sometimes you would awake with excitement wanting to know what it is that I am writing on you. The feelings would sometimes change the restfulness into inquisitiveness awakening at my words. If I told you, I would turn you onto me, and if I did not comply you would turn me onto you, the writings on my paper doing exactly what it is that you are doing, awakening to me gracefully, whispering to me what it is that you want, taunting me, making you awake with me, base breathing, squeezing with me. Kissing deep, penetrating me through, my tongue interlocked with you, written desires coming true again you are awakening me, allowing thoughts not said to be happening with you, not vocalized, but fantasized about you always knew what I wanted, what we needed was always awakened through thoughts materialized into-what is it the word-not yet brought about the word. The clarification of the sensations was always there though, still felt without vocal enunciation pronounced upon our being the feeling. You captured, we captured the words as they were upon the page there was love.

It is eleven o'clock the bells rang as I sit up on the hill, admiring serenity with the sun; again getting me through as thoughts of you come back. The dandelions surround me in a cloud of dust, releasing their fruits gracefully, guided by the afternoon's subtle gusts, while warmth embraces us. It is one of those days where I am happy outside, sitting up high, back pressed comfortably with the grass, papers recording memories wanting to come back. Scratching of the days we sat up on the rocks; we balanced them up high while the tide was out, in our bare feet walking through the mud, while the sun was bright, and the wind calm. The vast distance in front relaxed us, musical waves inspired us to create sounds of our own, mesmerized by the tones; I just want it back, you know. Sitting on the rocks, now alone, sadness keeping me up with you, writing to get through! Seeing you each time I close my eyes, images of you so clear to me. Remembering your smell as the breeze draws it nearer to me, the chills still burning, wanting to kiss you once again, your lips my lips pressing, breaths together with yours, my body it pours on top these waves; going back to those gentle days, it pains.

Especially as it beats upon the pane, I feel the loss of you, remembering your heart beating with mine against the rain; feeling exactly the same whilst you were against me. Listening together the rain no pain then, it is with me now, these memories somehow the same with you, sometimes are difficult to get through. Relaxing as usual, sometimes difficult thinking about you, in the rain, in the darkness weakness showing through, beats now under the rain, the sounds have definitely changed, yet the beats of my heart feel the same, just lowered now. Since you have been gone, they sound the same, in my heart I feel the same, the beats just now not on top of the rain, on nights like this it pains in the darkness feeling the same.

Yes now I remember! It is springtime's sprightly weather, the time where everything seems to be sweating with excitement. Water gently dripping down newly arrived blossoms, sliding down the green, bringing about an enlivening sensation to the season.

Deciding which seeds to be planted, flowers arriving
back on their own, baby birds have grown, arising to
their song to plant the day. Oh how we loved spring!
From its early brightness, to its long evenings, birds all
day singing; feeders filling, spirits blissfully together.
Basking in the weather. The creation flowered here too,
how it did as autumn drew, sitting...inspiration with
you, with Jasmine penetrating through. Under again the
shade upon wet blades, of our desires it was creation up
on the pages, painting, and writing of the days. The
colors...you chose me perfectly, my words uttered
precisely here too. Shivers in the morning, moaning,
Springtime's recreations working through; the realness
sometimes concerns me though, difficulty with the
words; overwhelming emotions materializing, moments
somehow true, reminding me of you today, as
Springtime's liveliness inspires me through.

The flower's petals smooth, and soft, their presence
we enjoyed all year round, I still do. Three leaves
enclosing them, opening up slow, brightly blossoming,
showy petals filling the season. They enhanced
springtime's captive ness, the growth invigorating,
walking amongst them after the sun has lightly
showered. It is just so relaxing, the memories of the
days, selecting a spray to use, the different colors we
would choose sometimes still rests up on the mantle,
candles surrounding them; calla lilies, black magic roses
all together flattering.

Admiring the seeds we planted; today...it is okay
without you. Love lies bleeding; planted ropes of red to
bloom...its deepness reminds me of you, ready to burst
into flames still looks the early splendor surrounding

our domain. The lushness is the same each year, the
flowers consolation; their brightness gets me through the
springtime without you.

Our friends sure did love you; we remember often the
days we spent together, while learning, and teaching
one another. It was the similar-ness of our paths and is
that creates us family for each other, supporting one
another as we move the days. Oh the days! The times we
spent sharing laughter, and smiles while conversing
with each other, company in beautiful weather.

Down along the river while soaking up the sun, we
spoke of you today, missing the flames, the ones you
danced around your body. We miss you dancing at
midnight welcoming growth, dancing with drums and
shakers encircling you, energizing our bodies, our circle
misses you. The enclosure has changed, a fire replaces
where you once danced, where we continue to welcome
each year Spring we still play and dance and sing.
Images of you in the center again dancing flames around
you come back to us each year we celebrate spring with
you gone.

It is late writing now of you, energized by feelings
from all day and evening spent with our friends, feeling
you. Your spirit must have been there dancing we felt
you there with us, now I feel you here too, lying in bed
on your spot, piano in the background playing songs
you composed for me. The music in my heart has been
playing nightly comforting me, moving with the piano
sounds you left to help me through these nights. Sights
of you remembered all day long and tonight, the stories
you told to me, unfolding, holding them while writing

them; the sounds in my heart about thee. These nights
again lonely while trying hard to capture spring without
you, yes its daily inspiration gets me through! I love
these great memories about you, I just wish I was
writing them with you, how we use to write, and paint
to the piano music you composed for me, for us. I love
you and miss you so much. Those times under the apple
tree come back often; painting and writing with thee
again inspiration with you, these feelings back again.
The silence needed so that I can rest tonight, it is okay
the springtime's crispness is holding me tonight with
memories warming me. Remembering songs recalled by
music playing; in my heart the music has been playing
nightly comforting me; your piano sounds bring tears
back. Touching shivers that burn on me, while listening
to your words about me from thee...

'When I look into your eyes, it makes my heart shine
it makes me feel so warm inside,
because I am yours, and you are mine
when I sit so near to you, it makes my body melt,
a warm sensation tingles me, an electrifying feeling
never before felt,
when you caress me the way you do, I feel so out of
control
touching my body, turning me on, penetrates my heart
and appeases my soul,
when I kiss you, and you kiss me,
it causes my lips to quiver,
rolling our tongues, hesitating...suck
making my entire mouth shiver,
when we make love to one another
it makes my heart shine
it makes my body melt

I feel so out of control
I love the way we move together
and how we each explode'

   One last hug now before we say good-bye, you mean
the world to me, it still feels the same as the first time we
held one another...right before we started working for
each other, and before we got together. We were
congratulating one another after the first show we met
each other, congratulated every time like that, after our
hugs stayed like that. Its warmth comforted us. It still
feels the same after the mornings arose embracing
greeting the day, and after those times spent apart then
meeting, our hugs continue to feel that way.
(Hug me please tonight.)
Every time we went to bed since the first time we spent
interlocked so gracefully through the night, I want to
hold you like that all night, have mutual dreams as we
sleep, keep us together peacefully until you go.
Before you go my life was transcendent, every moment
complimented the easiness of our understanding of each
other. Relaxing peacefully. Hold me close with thee;
keep your spirit tight to me always your words so dear
to me. Our hug still feels the same. Feels like embracing
my best friend is you. Memories throughout my lifetime
with you
(hold me all night long)
will get me through the days, will relax me easily, with
music in the background listening to music from you. I
will miss you choosing the apples diligently, and
making your cider for me, the spices immaculately
always it comforted me, I am glad you left me the recipe.
I will miss you making it for me. Memories are already
coming back, you know I will keep them to me close,

and enjoy our life as images come back to me. (Hold me closer squeeze me tighter please.)
Always slept while embracing, continue embracing me tonight, our warmth maturing us, caressing you lightly tonight, while whispering feelings felt.
(I am definitely going to cry)
Tonight will be like all the others,
(I will have time to grieve)
your energy will remain with me, the memories you are leaving will inspire me, you are leaving aspirations from a higher level of life, I will bring them down to me, leaving the images on the pages as you continue to inspire me, this moment will come back to me. I will remember the point in time you held your love to me the last time, and keep it forever in memories of my life with you.
(I will be sad)
Everyday a moment will stimulate me, and bring me back to the days of pleasant living, and working with you. It will be difficult a life without you, but I will get through, reliving moments spent truly.

Yet again thoughts of you are flowing, pleasant ones of our growth, developed smiles throughout the path we chose, intensifying our love's hope. I cannot help the sadness I have in bringing back moments spent with you, bringing about a somewhat solemn mood; writing with dignified serious words. Deeply sincere with memories I use, that choose to come back, those once thought lost are coming back to me, of evenings we kept the music low, outside...the ambience filled the air with beats moved to, slow. On my back your chest pressing, hands touching caressing the front of me, spent summer nights like this undoubtedly satisfied under our tree. So touching yes the scene! Nature in the evening moving differently, the flowers still to a motionless theme, moonlight shining the air we bring, and fireflies hummed to the song we trilled. Your cider cool and sweet and needed to satiate after dark when it was too hot to be inside, made our bed under the sky, keeping the music low, caressing happily with you in the dark; on nights too warm to speak.

Writing now the words aloud, our life coming back to me, reciting moments seen and listened so closely to. When I remind myself just how wonderful you were for me, coming back these translations the way I need them to be, your songs have been playing again. The one you wrote while I was sleeping outside on a night like this, in a hammock I fell asleep with you writing on me' from your everlasting touch, your depth piercing through your eyes, your smile, that persistent glow, maturing yet unchanging soul and undying need to embrace life. You cause me to sing about thee, in the most mysterious of keys; bouncing joyfully my fingers write how much you mean to me'

More on how I do with moments caught up on you...it felt like perfect lasted so soon, always in the mood with you, amused by times spent topping you with me. Divine ecstasy slowly but sure, you caused my body to melt with yours, our wings exposed we soared. We poured together our love each time we touched we poured; I want you like before. Today I am consumed with sadness from missing the love we kept...memories tearing me up and keeping me together, pulling me back to our times. Call in pleasant points in time always with you; I am missing you so much today in the sun. On my paper I am writing again alone on our domain, feelings ranging changing into flashes of your smile smiling for me. You are seen the same as if you were here...you seem real sometimes when the sun is burning and I sit being reminded of your warmth; through the afternoon star you are captured on my page just as you were to me you are.

As night struggles for control of day and the stars finally appear, I am back relaxing here, the colors again inspiring tones to begin the night. Red through the orange above the pink that shades the mist that glistens the stars. It has already started to rain; rain was always so nice with you, especially when it was warm. Eating apple ice with you under the clouds; going back to that evening aloud tonight listening to the rain tasting the sweet flavors of another reminder of you.

Going back to that evening tonight but alone. As I long for you here I cannot help but to fill up throughout, pouring out of me the rain pours. My pen recording joyful emotions running through those celebrations I had you. I cry for you my love the same as when I held you close to me, the realness of true feelings past somehow still invigorates me, filling up the scene as I remember you.

Clearly you gave me your eyes sincerely, dearly, they pierced my soul and drew me nearer to you. Your smile smiled at me merrily really, filled me up from how much you shared your caring; so happy to have been placed near you. Carefully embracing me with you nearly, danced my middles with your hugs on me on you, danced you. It has been a long time's past since I

last felt you; unbelievable the days passing like this,
protecting its time with care. Enjoying moments of
memories of you holding us just whenever. It is this
kind of weather that relaxes my mind down the most,
raindrops bouncing off the house, memories closely with
me. I toast to you alone tonight, 'Here, I wish you were
here with me toasting about us, our passion and lust,
lapping that. Forgot not about the foundation that first
brought us together, performing the same stage. Writing
upon the same pages our determinism determined we
believed, toasting our confidence making real. I sip to
the love feeling forever as if you were Here'

A similar feeling tonight was due, of present day I
vowed to you my love, recited it out loud, our day alone
with me right now, easily getting through recalling our
day. All day today I flashed back of our joining lasted so
long, of your oath to me in song, what I wrote you
played in key, of words matching me. All day long we
were awake and all night too, contented confidently, so
happy to have been drawn to you, quite similar you
sang to me. And what the sun seen that day the moon
saw too, of a love so fantastic sparks combined together,
while I am thinking thoughts about you. On the easel
you painted while I wrote over you, our love showed
satisfaction through the colors you chose; I chose to use.
Reflection from the sun enhanced the characteristics we
have yet been shown, a well-defined union we fasten the
glow. Flame-colored variation was chosen to dominate
the scene, true colors of us blending throughout,
saturating through the canvas more than what we
understood you instinctively painted while I wrote
naturally.

In the evening the sparks changed or something, I mean they were together, but in their own space or something, pausing often to listen to each other, then back into bliss we drew ending together. Continuing then ending together, certain we were there together in ecstasy, same sureness shared. I have to say how much I want you here again, leaving me with these days apart, our first milestone remembered on paper you gave to me that night, I gave to you too.

I am sad all over again; I was trying to capture complete happiness, the smiles that are real, most of what I am. But I cannot help missing everyday was like this, words bouncing together today unfailing love. Our beginning much like the end and of the middle too, stayed in love with you. When I write about, long about you with me, our first celebration here with me now; I write vigorously to get through.

I dared not write of this memory those times before came back, the day we vowed to each other like that, that day, our anniversary day here with me now. Crying out loud for you upon the same rotation we made that day, under the waterfall; I was there again where our ambition was made real, the day we shared with others how we felt about each other.

The falls rushing gentler than they did that day, the sun brightly burning amongst our flame lit together. I was there under the clouds with my flowers pressing against my chest, the ones I chose the same that day to characterize you. I smiled as I did that day with you; the tears ran steadily as I embraced our friends, toasted to you again. 'Our love it lasted reciprocated, playful, joyful each day we dated. Here with me now toasting aloud of a union everlasting. A rise to the love falling upon us tonight, here'

My hips they arise again. I think in the evenings when I am all alone with you, and yet with the morning's dew the passion is here too. Feeling true desires all over again and when this happens to me, the total ecstasy that was there, the same feelings shared, cared so much about each other mending us together...I get all choked up, weepy with the burning, learning how to get through. All alone with you.

Sitting in the bath tonight brought back the way we relaxed the evenings down; around the same time most evening settled our minds to, where our writings drew about the day. It was especially nice when we captured winter's end, going back on warmth spent; it's been so long since then. The breeze carrying your moans recalls it, the tones around you glowed each day and all evenings. About the memories brought by samples of your smell, turning me on well I cannot go there right now, discarding somehow these pains in my center for you.

Groins rising yes again, there is never any preparation for when you come back to me, brought by a sudden ache remembering you. There is great happiness throughout the memories made, what I now have. So glad you reminded me all evenings, it is difficult to sleep going back to when you moved me again and anew, and when you said...I knew was true, you believed everyday my love for you. These memories honest feelings expressed through my demeanor, the jolts of my loins toying with me, it is all about the joy and happiness we would bring, rejoicing you quite often with me through the days. Spring is still here and I am thinking desires for you, feeling longing again for real. Some times are lonely with feelings brought about by the rise in my thighs yearning for you; I rise alone.

Lover come back home for your moans have been with me for too long. I think about it mostly inside, not because I am hiding these desires still arise in me about you, rising alone to you. On your spot made hot each time I summon you to come, remembering you with me; the ecstasy was real. Seems now you are here again caressing me, causing me to shiver. With no equivocation twas real the feelings here with me now what we had.

Just let me rest a while.

They are the sensations that surround me during day's break that puts me in remembrance of you, awakening slowly whispering to me, I would usually already be awake while I admired how peaceful you are, awakening each morning with a smile for me, your eyes closed but happy to see me. It was like the nights before sleeping happened all over again, head on your shoulder while rubbing your back, so happy next to you. Realizing your dreams as you describe them to me, including each other we awoke with peacefulness every time.

The sky this morning is a vibrant light blue, the clouds overpowering sun burning through. These feelings now have my spirit moving cheerfully with the breeze that is blissfully flowing. Of course I am thinking about you, you mean/meant/are everything to me, everything seemingly what I knew of you, from the moment I first met you, you met me the same. Our souls met together the feelings we always shared; we cared about the feelings pronounced words with true meaning from the beginning. We showed of love from feelings felt in the beginning. Loved one another long before we could ever say the words. I love you for all the times we shared peacefully beside each other, overwhelmed but we just had to give in. Rode the flow we knew where these desires would go beyond the most concentrated of our imagination. You told me I said at the same time we felt we knew we had to be together, forever as long as we were able to be; your spirit is still here, next to me with friends. We toast to you again my dear darling one, all gathered around. 'Let us give thanks to yet another year gone by here, let us end the spring together and welcome fall, raise our glasses taller at such a time as this. Bliss for years and many more to come as friends, here, here'

Our actions through our way of thinking, words seldom misunderstood, opposing of threats, and worries through our mind's intellect. That which actions preceded our words, yet complimenting words through our motions, reacting accordingly to the intent notion of our mannerisms. Conceptualized living life through our way of work, working life through our way of living, consistently combining the two, working together, surreally loving. Our work easily combined smoothly, the easiness of the dialogue flowing, and the music gently drifting matched the energy of you and me, combining work with the keys. The desperation of our

works growth, showing contentment through hope,
developing the scene as we expand on you and on me...

   Act one, scene one
A young Serwa is sitting with her knees pressed firmly
against her chest, positioned on the center of the stage,
her voice a raspy key, she begins, piano sounding,
abruptly.

   I don't want to go. I've heard it done, I seen it
afterwards, I seen it! The screams of my sisters, pain
streaming through tears; we all need it done to prove we
are pure, to acquire a husband first! He had to be sure.
The pain it doesn't matter yet to me it does so much,
nauseating. That will never go away, but it doesn't
matter here, close your eyes to me I don't matter here.

   Young Chunna is squatting at the top left of the stage,
fearful, somewhat tearful, rugged, her voice
rough...piano playing.

   It doesn't matter here when you're a girl, they only
keep the boys; they should have to keep their first-born.
All day I wonder all around, crying, frowning; nobody
smiles or cares for me, discarded so easily on the streets.
I wonder if they even think about me, dream about me,
and if they cry for me, like I do...I always wonder about
them. I bet she was a beautiful woman. I am scared,
scary, they scare me every day, all night long, and
loneliness toughens me, I cannot rest, resting awake on
the streets. I am sick, I need to be fed, but it doesn't
matter here...

   A young Kimeri is crouching at the top right of the

stage, afraid, the piano lightly plays...

Tonight, all night long, not tonight, why did I have to be born today, or any other day; they are on their way, five, maybe six, I don't know keep them away from me. I am so afraid to be here right now, all alone waiting for my spirit to waste away from me, it's because of this rule I've been counting down the days, since I was warned about today, crying, I'm hidden, it doesn't matter my fears, these tears flowing consistently, begging, please keep them away...not tonight, or any other day, nor night, you know I'm not even allowed to fight this is a rite, no let me alone. I am a woman not yet born don't let them take that away from me...never you mind, it don't matter here when you're a girl.

The three young girls are positioned on the stage holding hands together, looking at the audience as the piano softly plays...

I am Kimeri, named woman
my mother gave me that
it's power does not define me
I am defenseless
Serwa noble, no more
change my name
but, make it the same
let my name be equal my place
let's get rid this pain
Chunna
Bring back my delivery
it's a girl, a beautiful girl
'let's name her Chunna'
oh the joy I would bring

they would have loved me...
(Just as Chunna is saying 'me') they all end together with
if it mattered here that I am a girl.

   The parties were spectacular after these shows, drum
rolls excited us all, and it showed. Developing the lands,
expanding us together, we glowed, all growing together
enhancing, as we 'consider humans together collectively'
the celebrations reflected that absolutely. The music
moved us even closer together, drummers drumming,
key players like you, and afterwards we danced to the
beats of the drums and keys. It is what we all needed to
end those nights, moving together our spirits united into
one energy, it was happening, and we enjoyed the
feeling of human togetherness.

   You came to me in my dream last night unlike anyone
before; I guess that is because there was nobody before I
knew you. What you put my body through; I did the
same for you. I do not think I will ever say enough about
you...the memories must not end, besides I do not think
that I can, our beginning embraced our hands which
kept us connected since we met through to the end. I still
have your bracelet decorating the top of my hand; have
not taken it off since you placed it here. I continue to join
them together when the night is ending...my nightly
thought about thee.
'Thank you for finding your way through me, for all the
memories of work, and you loving me right, my dear
darling one good night' and then I kiss your picture.

   It was the type of love letter one would only receive
once, a real love letter it's true; caused my entire body to
jump, so typical of you. Moving me like that because

you knew, I moved you the same, when I spoke of you it made me love myself more, I do each day that passes while remembering you what I said to you, did too. I wrote to you lots before which helped in opening our soul's heart up, this is the first poem I gave in response to yours.

'The heart of my imagination
is the deepness of my soul
that brings this great love for you
more than I have felt before.
Every time I see you
every time I look in your eyes
every time I hear your voice
all your tender little sighs
and your singing,
every time I admire your body
these things make me want you more
the heart of my imagination
is the deepness of my soul'

Questioning my questions rhetorically. Sitting next to me both fascinated by the height of our intellect, not letting us forget. The quest was the same that which brought us together, no matter what the temperature be, we inspired monumentally. Every day I give thanks, you see there are still those mornings I awaken before four to begin the day. It happens more frequently after autumn's end, when warmth begins to fall, using our home to get by.

I am sad because the pleasures are all gone, your songs long past. I thought the words you left through love songs would keep me every day. Sometimes mostly

it is hard to turn you on; I thought I would be missing
you just fine.
The night tonight keeping me awake inspired by
insomnia once again; it comes whether thought of you
are up or down again. It has been since Winter came, but
it has happened in the Spring, and in the Summer too, I
have stayed awake all night for days as Autumn drew,
as I did with you, just differently now. Memories happy
feeling sad, I long for what I had with you right now I
sleep.

We did not make a sound that night until the very
end. It was special in love with my best friend was you
back then. I go back often recalling all the times shared,
feelings had; I now have without you. Sometimes all I do
is retrace the path in which we led, how all of us are fed,
remembering what we were born here to do.

It is picturesque still of what it was when you were
next to me, willingly we all knew just what bartering
now can do. It feels nice to be with the hope in which we
grace, feeling securely in our places. Things continually
changing now it shows up on our faces as we greet upon
the streets; we all completely feel as we participate with
the earth. A brand new birth for us all, answering calls
together, in good company together, every weather
there be.

Going back on our work it happened outstandingly,
the world with us laughing and clapping, lapping that.
Continuing with ease our beginnings met my eyes wet
with peace, still feels new. I never knew I could miss you
this much, your touch with mine on the world as I move
with our beginnings met.

Our love was always enough to keep our groove
flowing, our work going. Everything I touched on
before, but there is so much more I have to tell about
you, trying to get the memories together. Sometimes it is
difficult keeping up with all these moments, what comes
first of what I see is how I write it all down, it makes
sense to me.

I am beset missing the love we kept together,
memories tear me apart then back...being reminded of
fingers playing on me before me now. I have the
recording I gave to you just as you were about to go. It
has been since you were here that I played it last, not too
long ago. Each season has had its turn this year, now
exactly a year ago, while letting you go, just so you
would know

'I am surely going to miss you
when you are gone away,
there was nothing better than
having you here
every single day.
I am definitely going to cry for you
when it is time for you to leave,
there is not a thing that could top
the fun I had with thee.
I am certainly going to yearn for you
when tomorrow your departure is here,
the only thing I know to do
is hold the memories near.
I am positive I am going to weep for you
when your presence is gone away,
I would do just about anything

to have you stay another day.
I am surely going to miss you
I will definitely cry
I will certainly yearn and weep for you
when it is time for you to die.

   Yesterday her birthday was. We went together to
gather the apples up. I made the apple dishes myself as I
do each year this day. Our apples with one-pound sweet
potato, both home-grown, peeled, the apples cored. One
half a cup apple cider, homemade, one-third cup dried
cranberries, same made.
Boil the sweet potatoes in a basket over water; let them
steam ten minutes 'til tender.
Add other three ingredients to another pan, cover and
cook five minutes or until apples soften. When the sweet
potatoes are done drain off and gently stir in the apple
cider mixture, cook over low heat 'til flavors combine.
Done

   One tablespoon plus one tea of vegetable oil, six
boneless skinless, chicken breast fillets. Three large
apples, home-grown cooked and cored, a cup of cider,
homemade, one table plus one-teaspoon stone ground
mustard, two-thirds a cup and add two tablespoons of
cream.
Heat oil in pan over medium heat, add chicken and cook
thoroughly, remove from heat, but keep it warm. Add
apple slices cook three minutes, add the cider, mustard
and cream, boil it together and reduce by three. Spoon
apples and cream over chicken.
Done

Our friends joined me this year and brought their
favorite dishes, we toasted. I miss your kisses. Your
birthday wishes made real every year I re-live the same
each year, writing at least to you in pen.

'I long for your greatness
in every possible way,
I long for your beauty
and think of you always,
I have keen desired memories
warm tenderness,
I have this yearning
combined with bliss,
Happy Birthday Honey
you I sure do miss'

The salad came after dinner, it was a combination of
spinach, apples, and homemade dressing...I will have to
recall the recipe later.

We had a place for everyone, everyone in their place
as we sat and gave grace, thankful for our space, all the
years' dates. Your birthday with friends, gathered round
again and there was no end to the talk we speak about
thee, like an everlasting dream or something of the like.
Sincerely withdrawing you. Colors I chose to represent
strength, love and contentment as I reveal my gift of you
to them, captivating friends, as we celebrated yet
another birth past.

Writing unlike I have before, well yes, but there is so
much more than this, there is so much more coming
back, each moment recalled a new one's pass, then
brought back anew. It is with the longest love ever to

last, our garden has lasted; its beauty everlasting, a
rewarding task even now at hand.

We must take care our land.

You are wanted in the evenings just as the sun is
setting. Breathing in the freshness of the day spent
together, and stimulating the evening together. The
colors made our inspiration dream up on the canvas.
Sometimes I lie there naked as you paint the sky on back
of me, up on the rock garden in the stream. Forget Me
Not Bluebirds surrounding me, touching on the scene
encompassing with the Angel's Trumpets...you got
exactly the scene on me.
We allowed the paintings to dry where they were kept, a
lot in the rooms we slept in, mostly in the bedroom, but
as the years they past we acquired such a collection we
could start hanging them all over the house, they all
inspired us as we filled our home and cottage up and
gave them out as gifts.

This has got to end. I think because I am celebrating
your birthday again, that I went sadly through the day
and now it is evening time. I think I will keep it to
myself the burns now in my loins. It is because the
fireworks happened after the apple bake cake, walking
bracelet and bracelet through the same path that was
taken since created. Each year our hearts there mated, I
am here now moaning aloud, bringing back the
fireworks we gladly made. It was real always you gave
your love to me, without particular occasion, but
especially on special occasions I gave to you gave back
to me...I want thee, all that I see, have seen you in such a
long time, I long for you be for me now...the flowers in

the place where I lay you down, on the flowered ground, twirled you around. Smiling with your eyes closed, we have always known the height of our bliss, kiss, missing you...I beg you to come here.

Come right here to my face, I miss your face, touching your face smiling 'bout me. Never again will I touch your face with mine, with my hands, never again brush my lips against your skin, your lips no not again. I will never again hold up your chin and kiss you as I did, will not feel how you did...I will never again experience what it was like face to face with you, except from the picture I drew after it was taken, painted it after I drew it, withdrawing now face to face with it. I need you now sometime, or how, right now; your picture not now I cannot look at you now. It is hard sometimes or, it always has been bringing you back to real time. But I still do, I will never forget my memoirs of you with me. Back in our room of Sanctum Ness, I sit here and enjoy another slice of the Apple Bake Cake I prepared for you; made it every year on your birth.

Four of our apples peeled, cored, and sliced, 1/2 cup firmly packed brown sugar, cup and 3 tablespoons all purpose flour, 1/2 teaspoon ground cinnamon, tablespoon orange juice, 2 teaspoons lemon juice both freshly squeezed, teaspoon orange zest, 3 tablespoons chilled, unsalted butter, and 1/4 cup of chopped pecans.

Preheat oven to 375 degrees F.

Combine
Apples, 1/2 of the brown sugar, tablespoon flour, and cinnamon in a bowl. Combine orange juice and zest in

another bowl and then drizzle in previous bowl.
Combine rest of the flour and sugar in a mixing bowl.
Cut butter in until mixture looks like course meal.
Stir in pecans and sprinkle mix over the apples and bake
until top is brown and apples tender, about 2400
minutes.
With little movement, with little sound, my mouth feels
like dancing, being alone right now I am chancing with
this cake. I made it especially for us on your birth date,
celebrating through tonight alone...happy birthday.

I think I found a better means to live for now without
you like before, without the pain that causes me to cry at
unexpected times throughout the days as I write. With
the tears though they bring about all the joy we would
bring, this is why I pour so much when I recall the songs
you would sing. Be for me now, before me now I have
what I have always had. You left but did not leave me
without the energy still carrying me throughout the
days...I carry myself with you.
There are going to be times again when memories
encompass pain, it keeps me real, helps me to release
myself through you. Of course I am crying a bit again;
they are always the tears that smile when I go back
aloud, about the times of the laughter in the sun until it
goes down and rises anew, a new grand day. Smiling
because our cheeks were to sore to relax them down,
there was no reason to anyhow.

Down along the ocean front the day after a winter
storm, sun burning bright, trees making music for us as
the ice covering them blows in the wind. We always had
a campfire then, included our friends from the day's
beginning straight to its end until the campfire dims. We

would mostly eat and plan about what was yet to come, recalling other things we had done, you know how life for each of us was won.

On the pages it was always extravagant, consistently fabulous, our friends and us held it the same. This is what kept us through all those years, the toasts kept real, the cheers, combining our meals, the best of friends. I will continue to recall our lives together 'til my end.

Taunt me noonday you would often awaken me saying that, your left hand steadying my body as your right moved over me. All on me, but you did this when you could not stay home that day, just I could stay; said that when I was all alone for the day 'call me and taunt me again' So that is what I did every time you asked me to, because I always got you to return the favor too, turning on with you. It was creativity that kept us together, made everyday feel new, just by remembering the first stages together with you. Made a vow to last to the end like that, over time it grew deeper just from taunting each other like that, every time we asked. And when we did not ask we moved and steadied our bodies the same, kept us in love as best friends; I miss you again.

I just want to bring back the mornings we would bring singing about the day, 'Good day today darling one, good day' Just like every other single day, no matter where we lay that night we called out to welcome the day. I really miss living waking like that; of course I greet the same, I just need you back, your back pressing against mine in the morning, then facing kissing the day.

The tides with the smallest rise and fall even those

relaxed us all, especially when in full, which they
normally were past fall. I am back here listening to the
ocean's call for me. It is amazing the happiness that
comes by way of doing good, by doing what we should,
everyday all we could. How fantastic the feeling when
dealing with contentment, all the energy kept us, is
keeping us together, calming the weather...acting what
we must. For real the memories keep us as one, it was
really not the end. We have always known the height of
our intellect that which has grown; all year the sun
inspires growth. We always hope it comes true, we hope
because it is right, we all live our passage to rite, writing
it all down ritually which keeps me going. 'Human
Kindness' path flowing not slowing down; a consistent
path chosen day after day; ending every night the same.

The sky now a vibrant red as I mark against the dawn;
it has been a while since the color of the sky was like
this. I remember a past time I was inspiring with you, a
now sporadic memory flowing through my mind.
Yearning to reach the end. A friend is gone. It is almost
as if the ashes are creating the color of the dawn; I am
not sure if I should write about in song with your music
throughout. Similar expressed feelings I read to you
after I wrote about you gone, this loss has set us static
stature for now, allowing grief to work inside, then
subside alongside me.

Today our friends gave thanks to another spirit gone
again, similar feelings to when the day you left us came
around. We sang the same song today aloud brought
back the same; the color of the sky now changing to high
red as I weep about, two spirits now dancing about in
peace. They were always the right moments we would

keep to move us flowing, the peak of us growing.
Healing righteously, now our dreams have changed,
passing on what sustained us whole, what we had along
as friends, releasing another spirit to our realm of
spirituality, the highest of us known. Using you both as I
write and hum, crying to you two combined.

Morning awakens me with singing birds next day,
back down by the water again; the haze above the clear
blue water in front of me relaxes me as if it is evening
time. The sun glistens slightly above the water as if stars
are blinking on it, writing that in order to capture
exactly later on the canvas tonight.
I have to go, the waterfall I visit especially on Sundays
but not for sure is waiting for me. Today is the
beginning day of our weekend, the biggest star's
brilliance once more animating me, the roped sweet
grass planted smelling nicely the setting, settling me to
where I need to be before I go. Establishing tranquility of
mind before I go it visits me and every time I am
reminded I go and drum and chant under the fall.
'AH, AH, AH, AH, AH, AH, AH' over and over, and
over and over. Remembering the calls of us together,
calling out for everybody still this day.

You are needed in the afternoon when the sun is at its
brightest; awakening to the fresh air together and slowly
stretching to the sounds of the falls; the echoes of our
calls called back to me this day. Burning sweet grass
again. It is a combination of it with the drum, and the
sparkle from the sun, that caused us to call out more, I
call more. 'AH, AH, AH' more and more. The feelings
just like before came over me today, I wish you could

have stayed longer with me, as I do of our friend.

I need you just after the sun is cooling, when the
moon begins to shine, I need this time too. All afternoon
into the evening spent maturing with you, I need that
back and those times in our field too.

The central part of our fruit lied off center our field;
shielding us enough from the sun to cool us enough.
Quite often we would be out 'til the day was done, went
in while the moon was at its highest and its brightest
too. It made sense to do in the summer while the days
were long and warm, birds amongst the warmth
warming us more with their fluidity and tones.

It makes sense to recall warmth now for it is quite cold
tonight...it was the central part of our growth that kept
us through the seasons, no matter what the temperature
be. It was the center of our core that kept us awake all
day even as we sleep, excited because next day we felt
the same.

'Good morning to tomorrow' we always knew so we
would say, 'good day to the days done and those to
come' It is a yarn now I live similar alone, writing the
narrative, quite often in tune. I have been awake a long
time now and it is as if I am losing time again, going
back exactly how we knew to act upon everybody, up on
each other.

The pages are coming together about you, on me, and
of the others too. Evenings like this I love writing on the
peak of what we once had and who we are and how far
we have come. The definition of contentment now

known to be real, changed that to where it suppose to be...remembering where we come from.

Now that the night has begun I sit here with the candles burning in the blanket I made for us. I write on a combination of all our Spirits combined, combining the knowledge we all believed. It is the beginning of the earliest morning and has just started to rain. The drops on the window remind me of the droplets of rain we made look on the canvas, the nights like before when the fireworks happened. They are happening again.

The simile encircles my body like the rain I pour, from my entire center I pour tonight, not fighting that, lapping the way we lapped together I lapse alone. In tune with my groins, my loins they rise in tune, it is much like when first encountered and of our middle point in love also. Not letting that give way. I enjoy releasing all of my feelings that come about while I am mindful of you, of our friends too I write about. I alone calling, backing feelings felt I feel in the moment...I enjoy this. Bringing forth the groaning throughout my body still roaming about, it feels similar now to all the evenings we brought back these moans united soulfully...

...just let me read me.

Chapter Two: The Blue Birds and the Fish

I am not too sure what type of birds they are, but I often paint them while they pose perched on the rocks, resting on branches, flowing together in flocks. Listening to the calls of them, the baby birds sometimes found it hard to keep up, they sometimes stumble as they work with the encouragement of the wind and the enthusiastic echoes of the skilled ones keeping together with the wind. There are ones with brilliant deep blue pigment, the most vibrant of ultramarine, an intense glow from the sun enhanced their beauty as they perch, posing for me as I sketch. The blue always brought serenity that was inspired, capturing details quickly as they move about so gracefully, quickly. I fill in the outline of their beauty as they frolic about, with descriptions that seem to match the quality of me, as I sketch their attributes to the characteristics of the sea, and with the clearness of the empyrean, brought together with the sun...creating niceness all around. The fish sometimes won't bite, it doesn't matter much though, it allows for contentment while resting on the tranquil sapphire water. Rod tapering, nestled snugly in a makeshift holder of rocks. The absence of fish allows for thoughts to become clearer, flowing as effortlessly as the wind guides the water. Sometimes the oceans rage is so mighty that it moves me in a different way, plays music with a booming sway through its depth, waves crashing and splashing to the energy of its depth, together we move...

It felt as if the waterfall was falling inside of me, not

stopping that flow; standing there excited about what I was going to be able to write. Not letting go. A long time ago I relive each time; I recall for as long as I remember the first time we came to visit, oh how it makes me excited going back to the waterfall. We felt as if the waterfall was falling inside of us, falling down, saturated the rocks while the water splashed around, producing copious love. It was tranquility of our mind, spirit, and body embodying all that dances about inside, surrounding our home. It is embedded in the fibers of our souls, no matter where we go...where I go, or where we went, it is knowing the art of time and how it should be spent, spending time with care.

I will not forget my love I vow upon these falls, I will not dismiss any part of you my dear, I declare now and each time I come to the falls. Things may not always come out clearly, but that don't mean I won't work through, I will do whatever it takes to remember you, no matter the days; they quickly pass through.

You had me when you sat at the piano. Then when your lowest note struck my highest peak, you had me there too. It was the entire time I first encountered you tickling the keys that I was pleased with you, could see all the work we could do: worked quite well at you, at me. In the beginning you could see we were drawn together for one reason. I had you at opening line, 'There is purpose for life given to all around' we shared...I had you there when we first met, we met the same, I never took my eyes off you from the time they first introduced your name and you looked at me the same when they first spoke of my name.

It is all the good things of yesterday that matter, healed spiritually all the pain, our work the same, called out earnestly each name we knew and grew from that. It was keeping what we wanted from the beginning that mattered most each day and all evening, so we grew from that to help us grow. It was knowing the value of our soul and how we all feel as one to keep our energy as one.

When you came you came directly at me, I givith that path back to thee too. There was nothing better than the world with you, celebrating, toasting wine thinking about each other...we all want the same. Peace be with us we all need love. We love eating. Food is something we all had to be given, had to do something about. I have decided from this point on I will be writing all of the time. Who knows, I mean we knew; love like this honestly came through in the end when we all grew tired, woke up and knew we had to do something about it. Healed spiritually together all around on our earth, a new birth we dance, no more chance for pain, a gain for us all, no souls left behind no matter who you be.

During the day every day we took time out to be creative, or we created in the evening as long as at some point we celebrated our talent...our private talent. Next to the apple tree we planted we lay upon flowers picked from our field, enjoying our middle meal together looking around for what to color. You colored...me too colored, mixing in the scene on me as I did you, took turns posing, or sometimes creating at the same time, colors blending throughout.
'Our Burning Desire Under the Apple Tree' was about 'you and me' captured specifically all that blossomed

clout. Enjoying eater raw each time we visited, pure and sweet; we particularly enjoyed the cider recipe (I now keep) you made on days under the tree. On hot nights you kept your cool with me, painting me in the evening under the blossomed tree.
When we created at some stage in the dark time we used bamboo torches to light our pages, and to highlight you and me. We used the moon and the constellations for the background scene, under the apple tree at night with thee.

Painting about, running about the field; one of my favorite paintings hanging of us all in our field, sitting on blankets I made for us, enjoying eater raw, and a couple sipping cider. You are gathering apples up in a basket, I have my hands in the flowers; a few birds soar above us, and one of us is in the water 'Flowered in the Field with Friends on the Field.'

As I lay falling asleep at night, your music could relax me enough to fall to peace. It normally invigorated me to come and sit behind you; hands on your hands all over you as you play. Getting up to write or paint on what I see before me there was you. It was the deepness of your throat to its highest key that created inspiration for me, singing joy, slowly, and sexy about. Playing on a private stage. It was the way in which we swayed, smoothly, that made the benefits come about, benefited us all to hear you play.

The photo album during the thunderstorm keeps me as often as they come; I always pull it out then, a tradition we done.

The pictures of you at the piano turn reminders booming throughout the house...playing now in the background for me as I imagine you moving in the pictures and everyone with you. Smoothly up and down the keys, singing as smoothly as you flow; it was the variance in your throat that kept our eyes to you, feeling your groove moved us with you up and down the keys, to your voice. Your heart and fingers singing about joy, hope, peace, happiness, love, it all filled us as we listened so closely to you. It benefited us all to hear you play, all eyes on you, mine on you now with the photo album you gave me to keep at arm's length during storms.

The words of the painting speak clearly to me; taking down my thoughts exactly each time I sit and stare your picture speaks to me. Your back facing me, head right to the sky as the sunsets over the water in front of you. My muse now as I write about your cheeks rose to the colors of the set, setting me back comfy on the settee. Eyes on the moon rising and the stars starting above thee, the beauty of the painting clear my words for a perfect memory back to when it was first taken.

During the dark time it fills my heart sleeping on the place where you once slept, where mutual dreams were kept together, now alone. I am so sad. I miss you will never cover what I feel for you absent from my life, what we had. I am sometimes sad going back on our ways, remembering each day we were together, in perfect company for each other, no matter what the weather was. It is during the dark and when it is storming that I am most afraid to be alone, the restless nights spent a little differently lone.

I miss the pacification felt when the lights went out, and after waking up. Some of the best memories kept are the ones we spent caressing one another to the beat of our souls combined. When our thighs were side-by-side, each night our bracelets touched; those times had in and around our home going back touching through the day, and all evening I miss the most on nights so stormy you cannot sleep.

I miss massaging your feet and rubbing your legs, I miss you doing the same. I miss you rubbing my shoulders...around my blades, my hands, my arms, and those points on my head. I miss the sensation felt doing the same for you, especially on those nights the storm turned off all light, like tonight it has woke me up alone. Going back in the dark time massaging my own head, in bed on the spot you kept warm for such a time as this.

I have kept under my pillow for years to read sometime before I go to bed or after sleep, the quote book we put together to keep us through the years. It brought us to fill our eyes up as we heard the realness of the messages that contain it. Took turns reading to one another during the awakens of each morning, 52 for each week for the year. Demonstrated each day of the year to prepare us for what was ahead of us there was the world.

We trusted one another as our souls inspired us to, did the work we were meant to, you loved me and I love you for real. Life is a big deal; we lived with our spirits kept us for real. For real the smiles were real, the chatter true, life finally shows promise for all, so true. For real we have healed spiritually the hurt, hunger, harm, no longer for real, for true real dealing with each other.

Reunited we move, there is really no other way to go about in the world, happy boys and girls, which contented us later, no more delaying our growth. It was relying for real on the hope in which we knew would come, that which we took part in, and therefore benefited from.

Not forgetting a soul we journey about as one.

The combination of your music and my plays joined with so many around the world, the messages of our friends combines beautifully through to the end, and every day before that too, and all that is ahead. We always knew what we wanted, what we needed was right here all along, through the music of song, through the message of plays, everyone finally combined together to change.

This story brings together how we all are, what we all do, how we love, who we are, where we come from and yes we figure it for real. Life for real we all know now, and have finally healed.

This story is of you and how you combined with me, and how I combined with you and us with our friends and the world all together, but mostly it is about us and how we thrived, felt alive every moment we were alive together we stayed together in true love. We were one of the longest love to have ever stayed, I miss you my dear darling can you come back to me.

The passion from my younger times has kept me through the days, just more intense as I grey my body down am I feeling...well added friskiness I guess, no I know. I am moving closer to your soul, your spirit. I feel more near you and it; well you are it, I will never forget, I want and need you all the time.

I am much older today from the day you left, my organs are much more intense as I get around at a much slower pace. Different from our step before, everything takes a different time now, still using it with care, carefully walking about at a cautious rate...to the beat my heart seems to be pumping.

Guiding my way. I have more time to write again, keeping the memories flowing, withdrawing pictures shared, words captured, so matured now.
I remember reading and not aware of the time, singing for who knows how many hours past; they were unaccountable in the moments past, too tired to worry 'bout now.

Let me go back; good thing I write everything down, archive all feelings shared, researching now to share. We were far from strangers when we met; we kept trust splendid through our eyes, our hugs, from making love. You found it so hard to keep your eyes on me even with everyday that past.

Our hugs stayed the same...every day, called each other the same throughout the night as we slept. We were far from strangers in our souls that helped us grow, kept us sensitive to our knowledge. I will forever relive that which like-minded us together, account responsibility we knew to grow from that. I am much older now, yet I do not seem to forget a moment past, they were too important to, we valued for real. I will always be able to recall our dealings, healing, our field together no matter where the happiness be.

Across the water from where the apple tree was planted it only made sense to build a theatre of our own to benefit from, being benefactors ourselves, selfless through benevolent funds, beneficial to all.

A gallery on the right wall with a theme from across the world over it, the gangway marked with specific images to the scene, filled up more through the years; pictures collage on the walls of all the performers who performed here; the new ones sharing.

I am sitting in the highest balcony (the gallery) looking at all that surrounds me, faint shadows filling up the chairs, the dance floor, and the stage. The red lights on above our heads, spotlight on you. The food we would choose filled us up as we moved to the night ahead, looking forward to it for the way it begun.

You sung first to begin the night, and left us with something lingering on us. I remember those particular songs...your voice, no music in the beginning then slowly down and up the keys. I am sitting in the gallery enthralled with thee, setting off the end breaking it down, up and down the keys vigorously with your moans, your deep tones. You have me to this day (even tonight alone) wiggling, jiggling in my seat, with candles burning I eat, pump my shoulders in my seat to you, jump to my feet moving my seat opposite my shoulders

swaying to you. Even tonight. I have you loudly in the
background shaking me tonight just let me dance alone.

Exploring the mountains of an extraordinary land,
climbing up to a vast distance of water in front,
smelling, breathing in its nature as our guide went back
on this land and its sea. This expedition was for me, my
anniversary. Rejoicing of my birth, celebrating with
drums and shakers shook us again.
Sitting in the center of the bay catching ripples going by
at our heels massaging our soles, eating a snack we
gathered in a basket. We found it comfy sitting where
the water bends on the rocks now exposed from the tide,
planted our feet in the warm mud, reflecting with the
sun.

Apples, apricots, cherries, peaches, gold in the water,
people live longer! Looking over the water looks like a
triangle. Sleeping in a Shepherd's hut on a monsoon belt,
glaciers crashing down, it rains so much! Walking
through the valley as green as green, lush land long
mountain chain.

We captured pictures all day, all night the entire time
there for my birth, drumming 'Merry of your Start' that
song replays in my heart, on the recorder you brought
along on my birth again. Shaking on the land, holding
fingertips together, how I long for my birthday again
with you, with the spirit of that land, your apple pie, our
bracelets touching...merry of my start.

I feel it getting warmer around my chest as I pull the
apple pie out of the oven, it is my anniversary and I
have got to make it. I feel the ache in my belly for thee,

the one all years I feel, I try to make it every year, the
sweetness of my anniversary here again how...
Time sure does pass; I remember as if you are here, you
still awaken as if you are next to me, where; in your
chair, the nice flavors I tasted in the field...in a pool of
mixed rose-petals because my birthday is here. Horse
drawn around the lake to the theatre, playing for me up
on a private stage looking down upon thee dancing,
shaking, moving my shoulders, naked. A deeper
moaning, base breathing, squeaks oh how the
celebration of my birthday with you I miss.
'I wish for continued happiness love and peace for all'

I miss you like the first night you were gone, spent
the complete day with our friends, the evening alone. I
miss you come back to me.
You are most important. I would choose to have you
back before anything else to have.
I miss you so,
so much you dear not know it.
I have missed you since you left, since the last poem
read, song said, tight hug, slight kisses. I miss you so, so
much you just may feel it, but I still want you back to
me.
I want the pacification felt under the sheets when it is
cold. I need to touch you again when it is warm out
turning the temperature up inside more. I miss you so
much.

At such at time as now, love day today my love is
gone. I probably should not count the number of years
went by without writing about it. A shame really, I have,
we had love day every day, each day a gift to one
another. But, the memories of this day too sad before

came back, grieved for your back to me, then front side of thee; I need that especially this month, but especially every one that follows.

It is like a part of me is hollow, not quite feeling full the same. Preparing food the same, eating at the same spots spent side-to-side, content with the memories filed.

It is just new eating alone, on our field, on our flowers across the water from our theater, eater raw and plenty of cider. Swimming across the water, rowing, walking, snowshoes, horse drawn carriage, sleighs; so many ways to get to where our work came real; sitting there earlier has now kept me up, at least love day has ended and I have the night of it now to simply sit with the songs well kept.

82

LOVE, love, LOVE, love, LOVE, love, LOVE, love,
LOVE, love, LOVE, love, LOVE, love, LOVE, love,
LOVE, love, LOVE, love, LOVE, love, LOVE, love,
LOVE, love, LOVE, love, LOVE, love, LOVE, love,
LOVE, love, LOVE, love, LOVE, love, LOVE, love,
LOVE, love, LOVE, love, LOVE, love, LOVE, love,
LOVE, love, LOVE, love, LOVE, love, LOVE, love,
LOVE, love, LOVE, love, LOVE, love, LOVE, love,
LOVE, love, LOVE, love, LOVE, love, LOVE, love,
LOVE, love, LOVE, love, LOVE, love, LOVE, love,
LOVE, love, LOVE, love, LOVE, love, LOVE, love,
LOVE, love, LOVE, love, LOVE, love, LOVE, love,
LOVE, love, LOVE, love, LOVE, love, LOVE, love,
LOVE, love, LOVE, love, LOVE, love, LOVE, love,
LOVE, love, LOVE, love, LOVE, love, LOVE, love,
LOVE, love, LOVE, love, LOVE, love, LOVE, love,
LOVE, love, LOVE, love, LOVE, love, LOVE, love,
LOVE, love, LOVE, love, LOVE, love, LOVE, love,
LOVE, love, LOVE, love, LOVE, love, LOVE, love,
LOVE, love, LOVE, love, LOVE, love, LOVE, love,
LOVE, love, LOVE, love, LOVE, love, LOVE, love,
LOVE, love, LOVE, love, LOVE, love, LOVE, love,
LOVE, love, LOVE, love, LOVE, love, LOVE, love,
LOVE, love, LOVE, love, LOVE, love, LOVE, love,
LOVE, love, LOVE, love, LOVE, love, LOVE, love,
LOVE, love, LOVE, love, LOVE, love, LOVE, love,
LOVE, love, LOVE, love, LOVE, love, LOVE, love,
LOVE, love, LOVE, love, LOVE, love, LOVE, love,
LOVE, love, LOVE, love, LOVE, love, LOVE, love,
LOVE, love, LOVE, love, LOVE, love, LOVE, love,
LOVE, love, LOVE, love, LOVE, love, LOVE, love,
LOVE, love, LOVE, love, LOVE, love, LOVE, love,
LOVE, love, LOVE, love, LOVE, love, LOVE, love,

83

LOVE, love, LOVE, love, LOVE, love, LOVE, love,
LOVE, love, LOVE, love, LOVE, love, LOVE, love,
LOVE, love, LOVE, love, LOVE, love, LOVE, love,
LOVE, love, LOVE, love, LOVE, love, LOVE, love,
LOVE, love, LOVE, love, LOVE, love, LOVE, love,
LOVE, love, LOVE, love, LOVE, love, LOVE, love,
LOVE, love, LOVE, love, LOVE, love, LOVE, love,
LOVE, love, LOVE, love, LOVE, love, LOVE, love,
LOVE, love, LOVE, love, LOVE, love, LOVE, love,
LOVE, love, LOVE, love, LOVE, love, LOVE, love,
LOVE, love, LOVE, love, LOVE, love, LOVE, love,
LOVE, love, LOVE, love, LOVE, love, LOVE, love,
LOVE, love, LOVE, love, LOVE, love, LOVE, love,
LOVE, love, LOVE, love, LOVE, love, LOVE, love,
LOVE, love, LOVE, love, LOVE, love, LOVE, love,
LOVE, love, LOVE, love, LOVE, love, LOVE, love,
LOVE, love, LOVE, love, LOVE, love, LOVE, love,
LOVE, love, LOVE, love, LOVE, love, LOVE, love,
LOVE, love, LOVE, love, LOVE, love, LOVE, love,
LOVE, love, LOVE, love, LOVE, love, LOVE, love,
LOVE, love, LOVE, love, LOVE, love, LOVE, love,
LOVE, love, LOVE, love, LOVE, love, LOVE, love,
LOVE, love, LOVE, love, LOVE, love, LOVE, love,
LOVE, love, LOVE, love, LOVE, love, LOVE, love,
LOVE, love, LOVE, love, LOVE, love, LOVE, love,
LOVE, love, LOVE, love, LOVE, love, LOVE, love,
LOVE, love, LOVE, love, LOVE, love, LOVE, love,
LOVE, love, LOVE, love, LOVE, love, LOVE, love,
LOVE, love, LOVE, love, LOVE, love, LOVE, love,
LOVE, love, LOVE, love, LOVE, love, LOVE, love,
LOVE, love, LOVE, love, LOVE, love, LOVE, love,
LOVE, love, LOVE, love, LOVE, love, LOVE, love,
LOVE, love, LOVE, love, LOVE, love, LOVE, love,
LOVE, love, LOVE, love, LOVE, love, LOVE, love.

'LOVE SONGS' to begin, from thee starting with the
very first one you sang to me about me called it 'Do You
Ever Dream'...I most certainly did!

Do You Ever Dream?

I think of you often
and I dream of you more
I have feelings for you
rather differently from before
they use to be feelings
ones you have for true friends
and ones others have for you
just because you are you..but,
| |: now my feelings, they go beyond trust
I feel love for you passionate desires lust
I don't want to quiet them, don't want to hide them
when you love someone
don't keep it inside well : | |

| |: Do you love me
do you think you can
will we ever be together, tell me when
Do you have sexual feelings
are they for me
I have sexual energy for thee.
I so often dream
of you loving me
do you ever dream
am I in your dreams : | |

My True Love I Have Found

Please do not think I will ever hurt you, or let you down
I will never leave you for another, my love found
things may not always go smoothly
we will get through spiritually
I will do whatever it takes to stay together,
I love you.
You will never worry where I am
I will not leave you for long
My entire being loves you
I will do no wrong
I want to be your lifelong partner
make that promise together
I want to fulfill all your desires
please complete me forever,
I want to be your life long partner
make that promise join with you
I want to fulfill all your desires...complete me, complete
me, yes, yes, complete me forever...
I'll do.

Now Angel

hush now little angel
do not cry for me
I have not left you for a moment
on our souls' destiny,
feel my energy next to yours
caressing the painfulness against the tenderness,
believe in our unity
keep faith that it remains unchanged,
let me continue to be motivation for thee
through memories, mirage and prepared ones of me

close your eyes forever count on me
my love will not recede
leave, there were too many great memories
hush now little angel
hush little angel
little angel
hush now.

I have occasion to be with tears in the afternoon celebrating times shared growing in the shade...further in the dark, what was made of love we had; all love is we shared. Our awakenings excited us as much as our evenings end, no matter what the time be. I enjoy those times when our life is very clear to me, when memories and scents combine with comfort consoling me, the similar kinds of pleasures pleasing me returning with ease on anniversary days and every other day.

The way we swayed. I continue to move to the same tempo to when the motion first began, still sending the same shivers through my spine, it is because they were around for years, the quivers. You know I am reminded every day of your warmth from your hands, your fingertips, so glad you were born; I wish you could have lived longer.

We were acutely impassioned for our days, embraced our hands most of the day and night as our bracelet touched; with love all the time. It goes back to the solace of our embrace, of our eyes that which could see our soul. It was knowing how to grow, seeing from the beginning, but waiting for our hearts to know and thus, the highest love was shown.

It was the combination of our motions touching, moving, my words soothing, you soothed me. Sent me into the greatest feeling ever to be feeling, this is why it is so hard to be dealing alone. Started out as friends before we knew my soul mate met you, our connection from the beginning outlook to be everlasting.

With me more than in body you kept me in mind,

embedded me in your soul. Day by day turning one another closer to each other as the evenings flowed. I miss watching the evening's control of the day, decreasing gently the sun as it turns the sky dark while stars keep the brightness out; this night somewhat the same with the stars gently appearing, sitting waiting for what to write. I long for all that a further, the little things we did to keep our spirits relaxed down, drinking down the cider, down by the water, weather it is up or down.

The leaves are all now settling down the last ones remaining but a few, the crisp wind has them dancing to the song they bring, the sun enhancing the colors they have changed. Some of the flowers are now gone, and the grass has grown just a little, the echoes of the birds has a fallen tone, most of the warmth cold.
I walked across the field this afternoon in the snow and sat across from the theater, made a fire to heat me, and drank cider to warm inside me. The snow is packed perfectly for snow shoeing, another way we got around the lake. Snowflakes falling, portraying a winter land.

The hinterland of our domain is controlled by the peace from within all of us, skating on the lake, watching people skate as we offer hot cider and chocolate, our apple baked products to bring them back. Gallivanting gadabouts in and surrounding our home, it was the comfort of our demesne that brought them coming no matter what the season was, arriving just because, there was a kind of feeling over us loved, so everyone benefited from.

It is the vastness of its view and was the lushness of the scene being used all along

music shared; it is welcoming with open arms for growing, combining as one. Keeping to the differences the undertakings to take on to make happen, opening our souls up in our heart. Bringing ones once thought forgotten forth to help them lively again, to sing in key, drum and eat.
Happiness we all share, really care about one another, having everything we need at hand, bartering in a lot of ways that we could, and can and therefore do. It is wonderful the land in which we live, Love I wish you could be here.

My Love,

 I will be in bed when you come home, get in when you can,
 I will be blending to the music playing, relax with me when you can...I will have all the lights turned out and candles lit, I will be on the bed eager.

 I will be waiting for you I have some things waiting, something on ice, hot melted chocolate and a many fruit slices, the music will be on already.

 I am ready, I have something I want to read,
so hurry on home love, I will be in bed already ready for you to come in... 'til then...Your Love

 I want to pour my love to you, from within my dreams make come true now. I am so happy I want to show to you what I am feeling inside, what I remember of you, did with you, to you, next to. Say 'it' to you; I have already started to write down about you, read aloud about you to myself about you. I want to rehearse in

front of you know how I feel, caress you while sharing
how peace my heart is from being joined with yours, just
for another moment or two.
Thoughts of you continuously run cross my mind, from
my head down my spine to where every part of me
begins to smile, my thighs they jiggle my knees from the
time since we first encountered...challenging my days
and my step, stepping me up.

There was always impact while learning of life and of
each other, turned on to this state of unlimited teachings,
reaching to where the possibilities could go. Sometimes
we hardly knew what to say out loud of our thoughts,
but we always created something new. Enjoyed the
silence surrounding us as we grew together, wrote
together, glanced up to smile at each other. I was
thinking for a while about the letter I gave to you when
you went away, told you to open it when you were on
your way home, a few hours away.

I was upstairs after the moon, you were traveling
back home, excited to see me, missed me, wanted mostly
to embrace me, kiss me. I was in bed just like I said,
candles were flickering around the walls, music
vibrating off the walls too, so excited to see you again.
Danced over to you and hugged, rubbed your back, 'so
glad you're home' The fruit we dipped chocolate down
with the bubbly, we missed so much we could not stop
touching, as if you were gone for years; I don't even
think a full moon came in the time you were gone, we
just missed every moment apart, probably from the
beginning without saying.

In my bed now I am laying, candles lit for the warmth

of them and the light so perfectly they grace upon my
pages to light my pen. The light fragrance of
frankincense mixing with the late evening air, goes well
with the piano in the background; I hope for now to
sleep.
It is nice, still writing about you in the morning (I will
have to save what I wrote through the night for later)
candles left not snuffed through the night keeping me
warm with thoughts arising up all night about you.

You were so difficult to look at; I could not help but
rise to you, I always wanted to kiss you, close to you
with my eyes. Aimed and reached with me as far as we
knew to go, why did you have to leave so soon. My
heart alone with this beautiful night gone by without
you, writing gets me through; the sadness works its way
through past pleasant recollections of you, our life
together.

What pleasant memories I keep! Even if a bit sad, I
plan to write them all down, each day and night with
you, and now without you, before I met you, and how
we met in the same way.

These memories coming on their own most times...I
want to sleep sometimes when my mind keeps me up,
writing so much so fast so scratchy, I write it twice over
again. I miss you preparing words to be singing,
swinging as you fiddle over the keys, while filling up
the grand staff, singing and humming your tune
aloud...made my words flow. *It is to be of the longest
poem ever to be written to match our love lasted.
Our energy grew. The more time we shared we knew,
slowly in the beginning, and then drawn in, you did not

have to tell me twice of your love I knew, I was falling in love too...before I knew my soul knew and yours did too.

Feeling as good as I should. I miss you come back to me.
Sad yes sometimes true, but because I love you miss you, still do. The air is getting warmer, blowing by me as I walked facing the wind catching my tears, my breath. Your face shows up clearly as I close my eyes sometimes to it, this is when the tears begin.

I went down to the gazebo and sat on the bench, sad of course I am. These verses express the excitement in loving each day like the first, quite possibly the last. And still, your name still rolls swiftly off my tongue, shyness our eyes caught staring, developed contentment somehow, joined the heat of our hands, my name off your tongue; and said with love.

I just need your hug.

You gave me everything I needed, was wanted. Music matched, matches the scene always, the exact variation down to every beat and every key. It is what I needed after down at the gazebo wanting you. I have spent time there since you went, spending time flashing back to what we done there; your birthday and other special times there too, this is still too hard to do.

You know to this day after the morning begins I sometime awaken to you calling my name, spoke your name as I awoke today. I have not gotten use to the empty spot on our bed, where we sometimes lived for

days, a lot of memories here.
Our thoughts calm, sexy, creative; I will never forget, it
was mystical quite often the way our energy stirred
about, writing about, smiling about you with me.
The images of your shadow will not fade from the walls,
fiddling the keys, figuring how to please. You pleased
me, appeasing to me, pleasing to see, to feel. I will never
forget my Love on this very spot and all over the bed;
you listening as I read, moving and shaking your
head...your shoulders too, got you up moving to me;
smoothly over the floor to the keys. I, I loved it when
you played with me, kept my flow going, passion
showing easily, easy to match thee as you played, could
hear the keys beforehand with your sway.

I read away, was blown away, your talent moved me
always; we said that about each other and of the others
too.
And of the others too they brought the same life we
delivered, that is how we got together, we were all there
that night and grew from that. We all had dedication
illuminating from our souls, was brought together for
one reason, to live life together with every season
change, birthday, holiday, and work celebration, we are
to gather.

We have been running one of our plays for the past
three weeks now; from the middle of the week to its
beginning. It is amazing the privileges when doing what
we trust in, believing in ourselves...I will be out
tomorrow night for good feeling, to our theatre built for
healing, the last night for this month, a week off to relax
our mind to where we can go again.

A birthday celebration to end each month, to begin
the next, all invited to come every month since built,
even if the weather is cold, people fill up the
surroundings of our theater and home, the inside of
what we have grown together each year keeps me.
It would be nice for you to be here.
We continue to live our lives as if it was yesterday with
you; we planned to for as long as life allows us to. We
continue to grow, to be alive, working a living
celebrating you through us, regretting your absence
from us.

Act one, scene four
Latoya, a Black Woman stands in the center of the stage,
her eyes deeply roaming around...piano lightly playing.

My name is Latoya, but do not praise me, nobody else
does. I am something that never was. No one has ever
cared about me; if I died it would not matter to you.
Don't cry for me I've cried enough for you, it doesn't
matter to you what I've been through. All you do is keep
me down, let me down, on my face one constant frown.
Don't cry for me you won't feel my pain, you walk right
past me thinking I am to blame, you just can't believe
that it's true, what I continue to go through. Don't cry for
me, you I feel hate, beating me down further, constantly
raped.
Do not cry for me I am too old now.

Spotlight fades from Latoya and at the same time it
focuses on Wuti, a Native Woman sitting to the left of
center stage...tears flowing piano same.

He slapped my backside and announced 'you have a

beautiful baby girl!' They have been slapping me ever
since, for as long as I can remember it. They do more
than that, but it don't matter, I recall telling once before,
'Don't be silly girl' PERIOD
That was it.
My body and no ownership.
Why the name
Why name me Wuti if it is equal to pain, if I can't stand,
it doesn't matter here...
even if that's what they say.

   Spotlight fades from Wuti and focuses on Eileen, a
White Woman to the right on the stage looking at the
audience in the gallery...piano still playing.

How long does it hurt, will this pain last
when will I stop feelings, feelings from the past
when will the nightmares end, how long do they stay
are they here forever to end my days.
when can I stop pretending, cry in front of you
when will you stop calling it the blues
when will I love myself, stand up tall
how is it that it don't matter how much I've fallen
Eileen, noble woman no more,

Spotlight
Wuti, noble woman no more

Spotlight
   Latoya, noble woman no more do not praise me; yes
rather praise me up, lift me up off the streets, a place to
rest, praise me to my best...Wuti you noble?
Yes I am. I am woman, strong woman, I must believe it
is true, it doesn't matter the past, I am with you, our

name means the same, Eileen tell me are you noble?
Yes I am. Noble woman raised up, we will soon get the
power of our name, call each other the same, the
meaning will be true...I have you praised woman, and
you praised woman too...
All, hands connected
It matters right here and now that you were born
woman Period

It was the development of our path that changed our
lives from that moment on forever. As soon as we
started to think it we knew we could make it, benefited
all who attend it, and to others around the world.
Creating hope in the theatre across from our home, we
loved our home, I still do. From any window, any spot
outside it is comfortable for you, happy to look at, nice
to be free. That is what it is all about, the freedom we
feel within our hearts, our soul, our body, our mind, all
grown. We glow and truly smile; the pain is healing
spiritually through real love, realized as soon as we
knew we came together to benefit each life.

I love the grounds we walked together as one; you
would enjoy this walk right now. The moon a painted
fingernail in the sky, you would probably be painting,
me down at the lake writing to this dusk. Drinking cider
or tea and snacking on our apple cookies or something
of the like, tonight is tea and our homemade applesauce
cookies, (I will have to recall the recipe later, both for the
applesauce, and for the cookies)

There is a peaceful calm in the air tonight, although it
naturally is, a delicate way to start to end the night, a
pleasant place to write even as I babble. It is nice being

here thinking about you, remembering you down here
with me many times before. The color of the sky like
this, the air like this, the moon that phase, drinking
eating painting writing you with you and me.

Tonight another night where I will be early ready for
bed, bathtub filled, incense and candles burn. Times like
this shared too in the bath, 'get in honey there is room
for one more' most times I get in I hear that, the first
time we ever did, the night we first moved in. The
shadows massaging on the walls, crystalline sparkles
blending with the water dripping down our skin.

Quite often the night would begin like this, down at
the lake, to the bath, then to bed, or maybe to the lake, to
bed, then the bath, or possibly the bath then down by
the lake. Made our bed under the sky; comforted
ourselves as often as we could, knew we had to...I still
feel the hands of you freeing the throes of life without
thee, keeping me tranquil, relaxing me tonight, sleeping
tonight, the memories of your palms kneading my body
as I lay drifting...'good night my dear darling, good
night'

We made great deal in our meals together, I continue
to even though it is difficult. I will gather flowers from
our garden in the morning, three for me, and then
decide which three to represent you. Always
symbolizing beauty spirit and the rapture of us, the tears
endure as I capture on the table what we prepared
together...how important each meal.
Including our apples as often as we could, picking a few
as I gather flowers, apple baked pancakes quite often we
would make, I eat now (I will leave the recipe later)

Roses, orchids, sunflowers and their seeds floating in water, in the vase you would often choose, I decided to use the same this morning to combine the beautiful rapture of our spirit still connected together, eating together no matter that you are gone.

The rain was always great for skipping about in our bare feet to relax down, to excite us as we pounded our feet on the ground... 'AH, AH, AH' to the pour down while inspiring growth and keeping the seasons green through most of the days. It helped to smarten during the changes of the seasons, which kept the year each year beautiful really.

Enjoying the gardens we planted. The chamomile is planted amongst the cucumbers near the onions, to add nice flavor, while the parsley and dill stay close to the Sweet William plant to bring the butterflies around, and yellow buttons mixed with them catching raindrops in their cup shaped flowers. We spent time here for hours admiring the seeds we sowed; bestowing comfort upon each other, the many ways in which we could.

We used our land in the ways its beauty intended us to, its lushness allowed us too. Welcomed friends over, and friends that would become, always pleased to have met in the ways that we could.

With the healing power of the lake as the core, we embrace the energy that encircles it, using everything around to stimulate me as I sit and do as we would, picking up inspiration from the scene.

I am glad you consistently reinforced our meaning,

keeps me strong today, the things you would do and say. The gifts you would give me on no specific occasion but for sure, always surprised me, knew just what to give me, to make my heart shine. Handmade most of the time with your heart, the music especially written and left, soothes my memories of you now; feeling how I always do when listening to your voice.

The way you spoke. Your words provoked passion that moved growth; you also said this about me. Said my words massage your throat and got you going, your fingers flowing; the work to not only inspire me starts roaming through your mind as I spoke. Telling the other not to stop, 'you have woken up motivation in me' I could easily see that, you gave me that; you were that and I am this; you are still that life to this day.

Mimosas awoken me some mornings with breakfast before I left the bedroom, (no matter where we lay) had us back for a nap by afternoon, to prepare us for our evenings. Oh, the so many evenings we spent together! I particularly loved the times spent in the theatre, but those times in the field and in our home, gone away and on the lake, I loved too.

I really treasure our time spent at the gazebo; we loved it so. I have gone only once before this since you were gone, it is just too difficult to venture...

Well, remembering falling to sleep there with you in my arms, if we fell asleep at all no matter, you would still be in my embrace, I would sit in yours. Mixed flowers on the floor; our place with open doors and windows, energy flowing throughout. Bodies soaked with love feelings saturate the flowers, face to face with mine kissing my smile kissing yours, spirits soaring to where we knew; they have gone before. I get lost down here without you, made it for you, planted seeds of flowers to take care for you, pick a spray and give to you. Close enough to the lake for you, comfortable for you and me, sitting close to the memories sad when retrieved down at the gazebo drinking mimosas eating breakfast celebrating with you.

As the sun starts to shine I leave the spot I made for you to go inside and prepare my day, it still looks early enough to be in bed, but too nice of a beginning to want to. I continue to get up early and stretch to the sounds of the birds, the freshness that the mornings bring is similar to late, late evening. Apple baked pancakes eaten down at the gazebo, went nicely with the orange-champagne drink and the memories of us there together.

Some of our friends will be joining me later today, sometime after the afternoon begins, so I have a few preparations to start to give great flavor to what is planned. Great fodder, and of course I make food with our apples in it, but first I should make the bread, that will take the longest. Then I can prepare the curried apple soup to slow simmer, and the curried apple butter can be made then refrigerated later for the halibut, the apple spinach salad can be made last.
(I will leave all the recipes later)
We were responsible for the apple products from the time the first apples blossomed, our friends brought their favorite dishes, which a lot of times went with a theme; today's idea is.

It will be obvious from our dress where we celebrate in the world, the music and the seasonings, the bells in which we play hanging from our fingers, from where we got our wine. I am excited already for the first to arrive, oh, I hear the bread is ready...smells so good, I am ready, and I need to pre-ready everything else. I will write later on how the afternoon was spent right into the evening with our friends.

It was early afternoon through to the evening as usual when spent with our friends, it is just after midnight now as I write, we toasted to you again. Brought great representation, everyone dressed up as planned, brought meals that matched; music too, went outside to dance and flick our wrists to make the bells sound, relaxed to the new moon and toasted you...talked, laughed, cried, you know the normal things friends do.

They were the words said then written then acted out that keep us alive. The quotes made real, the toast kept around, music and poems real. Kept similar hours in our creative flow, at any given time of the day we gave what we knew to give away, so therefore we did, I continue too with friends.

I fall apart with blissfulness each time I am reminded of you, which is rather regular; we were of the longest love, so for that reason it is more times than not, I feel not without you. Everything reminds me of you, sometimes I forget and set a place at the table for you, an extra mug pulled down when I am pouring cider or tea, reaching out to thee at night, waking up whispering your name. Flashes of you all of the time arise when walking through our field, when the sun is out, or, even when it rains or snows. I am reminded of your soul, people consistently remember you, and talk to me about you, and me, and what we have done and what I continue to do while keeping your spirit around.

Walking side-by-side, hands connecting bracelets, we also enjoyed holding both hands together facing while walking and talking, guided each other's way; you had my back I held your front. We took pleasure in the tree-covered area around, walked most often during the early mornings or evenings, with water sounds around. Camping quite often under the sunshine and moon rays, when the weather permitted, slept outside in a tent when raining or snowing, enlivened us more...we loved it when it poured and snowed!

The down pour and the lake filling up more caused our bodies to do the same, fireworks happened through the rain and snow whenever camping outside, under the sky or in the tent. It has been so long since I felt you last sleeping out to nature.

It has been so long since the last moment you gestured to me, 'darling come to me and sit with me' Next to you on the piano place eyes closed with glee, classical composition for me, the one listening to now, 'The Quest of Romantic Fingers' You sent pleasing shudders as you played, 'they have been found' had to have been playing about your own, they certainly romanticized while playing for me. All over the keys, some parts slowly throughout the room, other notes vigorously booming about. Eyes held closed, upper body moving, sitting on the bench, playing what you composed; imagining you just one more time sitting here playing in the key of which brought us even more bliss to bring us more together.

Remembering our second kiss, when we automatically locked lips again, it was routine from that point in time onward. I really do miss you beside me; I know there is so much more to write than that. It is just that everything done was done together; we grew daily together through our embrace. I miss us kissing, the hugs; talking about everything in particular for sure, with meaning and true expressed emotions about, there was hope from the beginning, and for sure after the second kiss.

After our second kiss that was all we needed to know we were for each other, especially since we worked together for so long: spent a lot of time prior together. That night we were sure, held each other from that point on in the single bed, far away from where we lived. Gave in, held one another the way we would for life, with support from our heart and soul, our body knew, our mind grew to where we felt as one. I just want to feel one more time your kiss, the one after we awoke, and the ones before bed; the ones disbursed throughout the days and nights, on different parts of me... while reciprocating back to you.

The drive home the next day was as spectacular as finding our way there, still raining a bit; the sun trying through the mist. The inlets often we stopped to visit, to take pictures; chatting breathlessly as we were driving, needed the rest to calm our nervousness, or rather what we knew of ahead. More excited as the drive persisted and we got closer to home. Could not wait to work together now that we were for sure, since now we knew what we truly meant for the other for sure.

I am sure the night tonight will be of me painting on the canvas, dark palette out to capture the evening, the white to dim the sky. It has been awhile since I pulled the paints out, in our room visited on Sundays for sure; sitting in the middle of the room looking out the windows painting the brilliant view.

I tend to start with the sky, as it changes so quickly, tonight though is actually quite easy; dark with a light hint of the moon lighting it...light rain? I have not included it.

That is it. I have decided to write a poem over the sky in red, use the acrylic over the oils to add texture to it when it dries. It is about the depth that lies within it, being a lot like all of us; it describes just how far we can go, when hearing all knowledge and acting it out. Listen closely when all else fades way...even if only at night. It is about looking to the light even when it seems dark, to feel enlightened always, darkness is deep, so it is about embracing it, looking further into it to make light of it. It is about exploring further from what you already know for sure, then digging a little deeper, and steeper until you find peace even when all else burns away...or seems to anyway.

We must learn this when young, time it passes at different rates it seems, at least we can keep the pace the same, heart rate the same, voice...find our tone. There is something special in the way we speak joyfully about each other; how we converse with each other from the time we meet. Not severe but sincere, expressions clearly

pronounced upon our being true feelings we feel. The
deepness real, this really changed things.

It really changed things when we all decided to work
together, live life together, and thrive from each other,
by connecting with everybody and embracing the
deepness that lies within all of us.

Dark time is not as often as it seems, although it takes
place each night. At a time that can be used to reflect on
how the light burns consistently, the sun and the moon
each day and night even when the clouds are in, you can
imagine seeing them, you have seen them before. I keep
them to reference at the forefront of my mind especially
when missing you, crying over the loss of you, because
of what we had, not because I am sad, really, but
because we would continue to live like it was our first
time together. That is what meant the most. We never
grew tired of one another, drew closer as the days went
by, really noticed it on our anniversary date, reflecting
on the year spent, and the anticipation of the one ahead
would be the same. Not monotonous, rather excited in
our endeavors, excited to be awake, and excited to sleep;
to learn and teach with you was more than invigorating,
more than enough to keep the years together passing.

It has been so many years that have past with you
gone, although it does not seem to be that many, like I
said before it is like you have not gone at all.
Remembering...
Not only remembering you but also sensitive to true
feelings felt from before, maybe then I do feel your loss,
but more the gain we had as one. I still feel the warmth
from you sitting at the dinner table, I often drift back to

conversations we would have, still prepare my meals the same. When I sit here I get an image of you while talking to you, as clear as the words you speak you sit in the chair, smiling again with me. It has happened before; this is why it is so easy to recall those times so long ago, so many have happened to bring forth when now needed, to breathe again with you.

To sit facing outside or in, taking in deep breaths together, getting warmer off each other, speaking words I still speak to this day. We would be proud with one another even today with added time, and take time out to show it; maybe that is all I need it. Sometime instead of images untouchable, I yearn to feel you one more time, which will get me by. I have gone so long without you, although my days they have kept me busy, but busy with the life we helped to create it. I wish you could have taken pleasure in it longer.

It is coming on summer and you can see it all over, the flowers have blossomed, the tree has apples, the land is lush and green...you know everything summery. Another great one ahead, similar things planned, more people around, lots of dinners arranged with friends. It is our anniversary, first light; I have thought about what I should do today for the past few nights. I will visit the waterfall as I do each year, but instead of having friends there with me, I will have them over later to celebrate. I miss you already.

I prepared last night everything I need to paint a present for us; the weather is perfect for sitting down on the rocks at the falls. I have gathered the same flowers to toss in the water as we did that day; I plan to capture it on the canvas today: to present later to our friends. Standing here I look and see the easel should stand where you stood, and I will where I did. My left hand now holding the palette up, as my right tosses matching flowers from the basket...ready to capture my present for us.

Our friends this year will prepare the feast as they do each year this day we celebrate at home, (when away we got together the day after we come back) I will provide all refreshments as we did. They will be here in a bit. It has not been too long since we seen each other last, we make sure not too much time has passed by: using all of our anniversaries and weather changes, and work creations to see each other. Friends surround sometimes not all of us at the same time, but all of us if all are around, at any rate, we did and still celebrate special days like this with friends.

It is refreshing when they speak about you, as they spoke I took note in my journal to include later. No different than the dialogue before, just more matured as the years past.
Equal to the number of years, I tossed flowers and uttered your name today, and the verses we said to one another, and then captured it with paint. The sun included as always as the background light of the scene, the waterfall representation of the way we vowed to flow through living; the flowers to symbolize how beautiful, just what life together would be.
I miss you. I am finding it hard to even write how wonderful this day has been, as odd as it seems I am tearing up again, I seem to be going back on my words. I love keeping you here where you were; it is just that the

house gets empty, no matter how warm it is, or the memories made; still making today.

I know how our other friend feels, our loss is felt the same; we consoled each other today. I wish they all could have stayed; I know I am usually fine, enjoy my time alone, I cannot really say that is truth this time. On this date you became a part of me for sure, witnessed by all of our friends, recalled back again. The painting has certainly captured exactly what I wanted; it was a good idea to use the space you were on to place the easel, I could feel and see your energy surround it...made it easier to mix the colors in.

I used the leading colors of you for the centre of me, the dominant ones of me in the middle of you setting off the colors in the water (the sun providing the light.) It is coming on the same time we kissed, I plan each year like this, to be here at the same time we wished the best for us...kissed the last flower and tossed it, kissed for that day, and the rest to come.

This painting will rest on the mantle with the same flowers dried in a vase next to it, until another year passes again, and I decide in the nights before how to represent our anniversary day.

I sit here on the settee mending the blanket I made for us with new patches. Choosing ones to keep up with the theme, our life's dream made. Another heart, inside a quote; next to it a course you wrote; a single flower with many petals. New friends' names to go with the many that reverses on back, a tradition used yearly to this day, to honor the new friends we made.

It is a beautiful day, perfect for your cider; I have also made some apple ice for when the temperature rises later (I will leave the recipe behind.) It is already a hot morning; I can hear it in how quiet it is, and can see it through haze. I will spend time down on the lake and use the blanket to sit upon, in the boat or on the field. It is one of those days already too warm to be inside, I will more than likely be out for the night, just outside the home.

Made quite often our bed under the sky, the constellations ahead, the earth's energy our bed, relaxed our bodies to where we could go again. I am heading back down to the field. The shade from the apple tree is all that there is, is all that I need to get me through all day, then I will sleep in the middlemost point on the field, if my mind decides it needs rest at all.

It does not matter if I do or not, the air cleanses me as I sit, the sweet freshness it brings blowing the flavors by, carrying the birds' calls providing me with music as I write.

The sweet music of the morning birds is as cheerful as when we were awakening together, as I each morning still do too, now, down at the lake with their music.

Chapter three:
Let me read me. Sitting in front of the lake reading
The Slow-Moving Islet

We moved this island together slowly; except during
the ocean's easy rage, that only happens when it rains,
which usually takes place on nights so relaxing you're
restful. I'm not too sure what type of fruit they are, but
each breakfast I go around selecting a few for my
nutritious beginning, then from some point on the islet I
enjoy it. There are many types of shells that grace the
sand, covering the strand right along the line where the
water comes to. The spiral ones are good for listening in
when everything else is quiet around. Here it is slow
moving, from the tiniest sea creature exploring the isle,
to the birds that soar above it. Constant summer for
days, the rain relaxed our nights on this peaceful isle.
I came across it somehow when I got lost, I thought I
was rowing south, but I was moving to the east, I think I
fell asleep and didn't realize that my direction shifted. I
didn't think to check it because when I awoke there was
a family of dolphins going the same way. The beautiful
blue, green, yellow color of their bodies caught my
creative eye and had me painting against the early sun
shining off them. I didn't even think to pull the compass
out as I was listening to their calls; the little ones keeping
up with the larger ones eager calls to them through the
breeze. The compass didn't even dawn on me and I'm
glad it didn't, I would not have landed on the precise
spot that I needed, 'The peaceful Isle, The Slow-Moving
Islet' moving me to where I had to go...

I have to go inside and get the ice, it is so hot right

now, the shade is cool enough, but I need to satiate my pallet. I still have the occasion of speaking out loud still today; it is harder to do while sitting outside when hot. I am so glad you left that recipe too, I promised to do the same.

A good swim is what I needed to add to what the ice has done, satisfied me enough to sit under the tree again. I just may close my eyes to it; imagine inside all that I see and feel from today, summer is here...there are so many things planned.

Of the moments spent this summer I believe the ones spent with friends to be of most important, since we got together to celebrate everything else that mattered. I was on the go quite often, relaxed frequently on the lake and under the tree, whenever I had time to reflect on me I did; I took quiet time out for me. I wrote, and before I knew it we all noticed the color changes starting, the leaves starting to fall again, less calling from the birds, and the days shorter again.

I watched the moonflowers open for the last time as tonight the temperature will continue to drop, I look forward to having them under most of our windows again once the summer rolls back round. We often made a wish in them, just as they were closing to be set free the next night, then wishing again, did that as often as we could. I continue to do now and did tonight. With the few moments that I had, I wished the way we nightly did when we were able to catch them open. 'To hold all who we know safe, others still to know the same, keep our love the same, please keep everything we hold in the world we cherish, safe' and it closed for the last time until next summer last night.

As I watch while sitting at the bay, out the window at the scene and how most of its color has faded, I take time to reflect on how time in the summer was spent; with all the color it had and use it in the months ahead.

Now that it is fall I am relaxed at night by the puffs of air through the windows open, candles nightly flicker light around the room from the light breeze. It brings occasional bursts of rain down, which really makes it sound good, it sets the mood good no matter if for sleep or to create.

The sweet details of our speech woke up the dreariness of the view, recalled inspirational things from the months prior to color things up. Lavender therapy from flowers picked before the season fell; sitting in the bath, purple color floating around, calm to where my mind will flow.
As I lay plunged to my neck, the water and lavender put me in mind of you as you lay on the hearth. I outline the particulars of your feature as you are positioned there, fresh lavender around, candles lit, wine glasses at hand; feels like we are down there. Maybe that is where I will make my bed tonight, light the fireplace and the candles tonight, scatter lavender, and enjoy wine upon the hearth as we so often did so long ago.

So often so long ago your hands caressed the particulars of my features as I lay in front of the fireplace, studying me; reinforced me as often as we lay; I did the same. The heat combined with light pressure from your hands will not leave my body, or my mind; they have not to this night...as I lay falling to slumber.

Three o'clock in the morning and a thunder and lightning storm awakens me; I was having a peaceful dream, of sleeping next to thy. It is in these dreams that you assure me that you have not left at all; there are too many memories to recall, feelings left behind to pick up when I need.

Your voice playing in my mind to keep me with the storm, the rain pours down and the lightening lights up from time to time the room. I have the candles burning, writing desires of comfort needed, especially during this time when it is storming out. It is this time I need you the most, the storm is nice to be hearing, but it makes the house cold; everything is turned off. This is when you would light the fireplace and make your cider over it for me; of course I can do it myself, I have. It is just that we used this loud booming to make music of our own, combined with the storm and made similar actions within us. Pouring so much, lighting up, our sounds in-between the noises the sky makes, I miss you next to me; I was sleeping just fine next to you and then a thunderstorm awakens me!

We are honoring your birthday today, I am glad you know nothing of the things planned; I love surprising you. Breakfast first off on a flowered blanket in the field, bubbly orange drink, and your favorite morning meal. Resting on the lake will happen after the field, this is where I tell you what you mean to me, and what you mean to so many; so happy you were born. Your birthday happens when it is warm so I plan to keep you out all day, enjoy our demesne...tonight dinner down at the gazebo and a camp out.

We walked down to the gazebo enough time before the sunset for me to get the grounds ready. You watched as I placed strawflowers around, comfortable enough for a pallet, my palette ready to paint you with the colors the sky is now changing. Enjoying wine, and a selection of fruit with simmering chocolate , I begin to stroke the page lightly with the brush, blending the hue to you, talking about you face-to-face.

You look stunning as always, getting a rise out of me as usual as I gaze upon thou, looking up at me with perfect beam, your eyes shine and light the work of art that is you on the canvas. On the bed of mixed colored strawflowers you beckon me to come over, but I have not finished, the background not completed; you tell me to keep it in mind for later. So I did, I sat next to you and you held my wrist, started stroking the colors over your body, and over mine.

Rolled around on the flowers, the hours past, the sun has gone down and we are well revived, so alive with feeling! Now enjoying apple cake under the sky, at the lake...so happy it is your birth date.

Back at the spot where the carnival took place for many, many years in the past, the Sweet William has lasted and has reached its potential growth. I can smell the blossoms as I approach it and sit down to bring back all the excitement this site brought. The crowd of people laughing, eating candied apples, (I have the recipe to leave later) the Ferris wheel ride we loved riding, but our favorite one was the merry-go-round because we got to sit front to back so snugly.

I remember the way you would hug me and whisper
to me, like the others riding, happy to be going around
and around interlocked with their love; included theirs
with ours. The energy from years ago still feels in place,
the memories not yet erased from my mind, no plan to
anyhow as I visit every year to keep them here. The
sweetness from the candy apples tingles my throat, as
the smell from the flowers gives me a reminder of that
taste. Moments like the ones spent here could never
escape to forgetfulness, there was too much love around,
too much fun for it to.
As I stroll away from the grounds for another year, I
look back at the close clustered plant and hope for it to
be here for me to sit next to, the next time I come back to
hear and smell the pleasures this place continues to
bring me.

Singing because you could, all the time you would; no
wonder you felt so good, bouncing the way you did,
sitting at your piano or not. It was the thought of
hearing the keys to your words that made you smile a
lot, caused me to smile with you. Creative stepping to
the beat, to feel the mood of the tempo, then to the piano
you would go. I cannot ever stop recalling memories of
the times you played. A musical brilliance with me, next
to me, composing about me, with me for you, for work.
I look around and it hurts to steady my eyes sometimes
on the piano, the one specially made for you, went
perfectly with your fingers your soul. Sitting next to you
hearing the power of creativity while working on mine
gave me all that I needed, or have ever hoped for.
Playing about me; letting me know what I mean and
always have meant, about times spent, lovemaking
kept...I cannot forget.

I am so glad you left all your songs for me, I play them consistently when it is not too difficult to turn you on. It sometimes is, today it is not; you have been on since morning time, listening closely to your words, your tones. It has been too long since the times we sat on the bench at the keys, it would be nice to have you sitting here with me, playing for me about me. One last time to see what first drew me to you, the energy you exuded while you played over the keys...my I sure do miss you.

A little of my soul left when you went away, I think that is why I get a little sad when I think about you. Maybe my spirit was seeing you off, sometimes goes to visit you, keeping me down here; then bringing me back alive. Each time I think of you I smile, I cry a little, I feel a little less full, then full with feeling. Constant dealings with missing what today would bring; work celebrating the songs you played. Today this morning I am so sad, I sure do miss the other morning times awakening consoling the days, to the music you would sing, the breakfast you sometimes prepared alone, the birds' songs, the break of day...those breaks through the days. The sun is just peaking in on the spot where you once laid, remembering how it lit your face, complimenting your smile.

It is coming on winter and I have been trying to happily get through the fall, by recalling moments spent with you; trying not to miss you too much, cry too much. But the truth of it is, is that I have longed for every single day. It goes back to the very beginning when we knew each other's name; that reinforced the feelings we were each having while the other performed. I cried way back then, but the tears were never sad, they

were simply glad always, no wonder we stayed together
so long; could write so many poems and songs. Great
company together no matter what the weather was. But
the weather this dawn is in agreement with the tears that
can easily build while it is pouring so hard for so long
outside. When it is dark during the days because the
storm has turned all the lights out, so you sit by the fire
from the cold.

   Drinking hot cider in the blanket with all of our names
for reverse, I write to hope for peace and growth
through this winter, bring together the other times we
spent together even when it is dark I have the light to
recall. We taught this together so I must use it; it does
not mean that I cannot grieve, I will release tears
whenever they need to flow; must mean that my soul is
off visiting you. That makes me smile, even if it keeps
me down down here, my soul must be gleaming with
high spirits; I just hope it always comes back; especially
when it is storming and all the lights have gone off.

   Always from the heart...in no particular order you are
recalled just as you were to me you are as clear as the
day is perfect.
The perfection of this morning gets me excited to get
writing, not a cloud in the sky, baby birds peeping, the
lake a quiet ripple as I get ready for writing. If I were to
start off again about you, I would have to begin with
your eyes, what first caught my eyes and kept me
fixated on you. How stable and protected you made me
feel; you felt the same, from the deepness our eyes had
in the beginning, and how the wind caught our breath
the same, no matter which way we were coming from,
our souls were suppose to meet. Your smell, the sweet

smell of your sandalwood turned me on well, hearing you croon, crooning me; I take your true sentimental words to hold me. Keeping me up now. The perfection of the days we showed to each other to keep us, using the rain as much as using the sun after the snow has fallen. No matter what the season was, temperature was, what was forecasted for the day or night we did what we were meant to do, I continue too.

So I would have to mention if I were to begin anew about you, that all along we made the most of our time together, disregarded it with care, kept to the pace we were comfortable with, took care of each other.

I enjoy the true feelings I am able to recall of you; kneading my back, but I need yours. I long to touch your body so much sometimes that is all I want to write about, anywhere sitting somewhere in our home next to you just one more time, outside, in our theater. Feel the heat from the sun intensifying through my palms, all over the outline of you, your skin, those whispers in your ear while nestled against thee, I feel your hands over me; I need to touch you your hands. There is nothing here I can hold that feels just like you, everything just reminds me of you...
Looking at my hand...

I have been so sad, I have never gotten over the day you left, the day I wept more than I ever knew I could; the tears really have not stopped flowing, I miss you so, they will more than likely stay. Maybe it is because it is wintertime and we enjoyed the fire together, I do not recall sitting here before on my own, not while you were here. Every day I sit writing looking at the bracelet you

placed on my wrist before you left, decorating both my
hands, remembering everyday that day together.
Making me smile with tears. It is because your gifts were
mostly homemade, so most things I look at I see your
soul in it, everything else you put your heart in it, I met
you the same.

I will never forget the way you wrote my name
interlocked with yours, the colors you chose to represent
the ones exuding from our souls, matched the painting
you made especially for us on our special day. One more
moment painting on the canvas, painting over my body,
or yours, that is all I need to get through the time I have
left.
With motivation left I pick up on my own everything we
did and said we knew would come back to us; would
keep us to the end; is keeping me up regardless if most
things are difficult to inspire without you. I love what
sustains me, it is like you are not gone at all, but you are.

I look up at the stars and wish the way we would
together, wondering if you are looking down with
tradition, wishing and kissing me, hand on my back
sleeping next to me, good nights. The nights were
always good for sleeping, the days we awoke with
energy, or sometime we used it up at night and used the
day for resting. Whatever the circumstances, or
surroundings, or weather; we worked it well together,
that is why you have been missed so much for so long.
Your music, I cannot help but to recall; I have you
playing most of the time to keep me going, words
flowing,; our time clear in my mind for work to
continue. I work as if you are alongside me, living with
your energy beside me, not a day will pass without your

smiling face, the heated space around you left here for me to be reminded of. From any place that I go you were there as well, so there are many more times to write about even if I end up weepy, the memories made to hold me up do keep me. Some times are better than other days or nights, but I could not be happier, but that means that I can also be saddened easier, especially when I realize that you are really gone. At least I do have the memories, they always help me before too long, by and by I will see you again, embrace you again, and sleep facing you before too long our souls shall meet again.

Our dream life was our true state, participated in all aspects reflecting what was ahead of us, what we dreamt about all along. I watched you nightly in my sleep; spoke to you the way I did while awake, and touched you the same. Rowed on the soft ripples of the lake, celebrated with wine and cheese and cake, and did the same while we were awake. Prated through the night and awoke with clear intentions, spoke of what we knew was ahead from what we watched while we were sleeping. Similar dreams you were keeping this is why we were brought together; we understood what it meant to understand life and living it.

Sitting on the dock with my slacks rolled up, socks off, toes splashing the water, rod rested in a holder, not really hoping to catch anything, just relaxing over the midnight lake. The moon is full, but it is hardly seen through the clouds and the fog that almost touches the lake. There is a calm tonight that I wanted to be amongst, the fireflies through the mist, crickets a bit, the light ripple sounds of the lake, the crackle from the fire pit...memories of us.

We were sure to be outside down at the dock just
before midnight when the moon was full, there quite
often was and is a composed demeanor this particular
night brings. Depending on the weather the cider was
opposite to regulate us, we brought pens and paper with
us no matter where we went, so we brought them along
that time too, paints and canvas just in case, food to
satiate, and great fodder always.

I recall in these late hours sitting here relaxing looking
at you not doing or saying anything at all, feeling such
true contentment no words had to be said, I hope I said
enough to you before you left.

Before you went we gave tremendous love, made it
with one another the same; ecstasy is real, I felt it before
and still it comes back to me. I sit with my spine straight
to where you raised me up, sent shivers up and down
my body holding me up. As such feelings arise I do not
hide them, I go with the motions my body flows, where
my mind goes, I am not rising completely alone now, I
feel you all over me, must mean your spirit is down
visiting me, keeping me aroused down here.
I hear your undertone. I love you so much; your touch
touches my soul righteously, here for me time after time,
whispering my name to me. You have not really gone
have you, making me feel like this, blissfulness rising
my middle, pleasing shudders all over, causing me to
release me to you. I love you for everything you did for
me, your love added to mine enhanced our intimate
times with each other as often as they came. We came
together to the point we were destined to go, our love

grew every day, held tight through to the end while loose to one another, taking you with me, me with you, together we came through whispering I love you with the other's name.

My heart beating as deep as it always has, I seem to be more sensitive the more the days pass, memories past come up as vivid as if living for the first time, in no order, but as clear as they were.

A natural connection, we met so young to live together for so long, I am often here, my mind wandering, wondering at the stars, I wonder where you are a lot. I walk across our field and find a spot comfy enough to reflect, as we often did. With the stars ahead I hope to see and therefore I do, see you looking over me. I love to see the fireworks the stars sometimes like to display, I hope they are for me; bringing back the ones we would moan through, quiver through, end but not letting go of you. It is all these little things we did over and over, using our creativity to benefit. Loving every moment spent in our closeness.

Repetition was good for us, our beat steady, our bodies pumped together the pace our hearts pumped, mine still the same, just lowered now. Since the last beat felt pressed against your heart I heard, the last beat we made together, it is so quiet now, except when I think of the solace of our sexuality, our spiritual unity...that gets me deep pumping. The fireworks flash back quite often in me, that gets my soul jumping...they must be for me, I gaze upon the display the stars tonight have brought, and immediately thoughts of you are vivid. As clear as when you were here I hear you moaning through your work, fire burning in me, and it continues to feel like you are here.

   This is one of the love letters you gave me, the first one actually. I did not think you could top what you wrote the first time, but you had this way every anniversary night of making me feel special. The type of letter one might expect to receive once, but every year you wrote to me in pen, on the same paper we gave our first year together and used it to the end.
It sent tears rolling, my voice low as I tried to express how it made me feel, filling me up more once I recall it, on our anniversary day or any other day it comes back.

`Darling,
   You are more than enough having reached me, pleased me and seen right through me with your soul. This is the first year we spent whole, I vow to keep my excitement the same; I always imagined this level of contentment existed, so happy you did too. There is so much I can already write about you, to later sing to you. I am so glad your body feels the same; soul feels the same, mind sane with mine. Looking at you makes me look forward to the days at hand, your hand in mine, so happy you love the bracelet I made, I love holding your hand. Sleeping next to you, arising with the same feelings in the morning, I love the days and evenings with you. You make me shine; I mean you truly make me glow, I meant every word I said upon the rocks at the falls, and I mean all the ones ahead. I love you darling, the anticipation of tomorrow keeps me content, every moment with you complements my entire being, thank you for your entire being, being with me.
Happy Anniversary Darling, the paper one'

After this letter we continued to grow, we opened up as expressed day after day, year after year in the letter you gave to me expressing what I mean to you and have all along. Similar expressed feelings from my heart to yours, soul-to-soul, and like-mindedness. I miss you the same as I normally do on anniversary days spent remembering you, or any other time flashes remind me of you. I miss you come back to me.
You left me down here strong with your energy encircling me, thank you for returning to me. I am and have been selfless enough, to be thankful enough for the times shared; I look forward to your spirit, beseeching you often to come back I feel your visit. You must miss me as much.

Keeping up with me allows me to continue our journey, my path now back to you, making it comfortable knowing I will see you again; I know I am sometimes sad down here, it means that memories of you are so close at hand, I miss your presence when I quite often reach out to hold your hand, hand on my shoulder, I sometimes caress yours there. I look and it is not there, but I feel it there, both hands comforting me, when I open my eyes you are not with me, so I keep then closed. When I dream and daydream I am with you, I cannot help but to, we were of the longest love.

I miss you so
so much you dear not know it
I miss you come back to me.
I miss you so
so much you dear not know
I miss you come back to me.

I have missed you since you left
since the last heartbeat felt.
I miss you.
I really miss you.
I miss you
come back to me.

This wintertime is almost over, the lake reaching its
fullest level, I have started work on the garden, flowers
have started arriving; I am excited for the ones we chose
in the morning to come back.

We were sure to gather the flowers before the frost,
for during those months the flowers are not around to
pick a spray. We dried them for the center display of us,
positive energy flowing freely, how we needed to and
therefore I must continue to feel and exude. The more
spring times that come around the more enlivened my
days become, by keeping the reminder, the routine of
drying our flowers as to color up the scene.
Representing what we mean, I look forward to the
flowers coming back round this spring.

'Come closer...closer, I want to play you
something...you are something else, you have my trail
blazing, amazement to me, but not my soul that which
brought us to meet that night. Off the top of your head
you glow, down your spine, your outline down to your
toes, your eyes your windows allowing me to see me in
you. Thank you.
You cause me to put music to my words, your tone
the most brilliant tone to know, raising the bright flame
in me. Seemly desires for me, word for me pleasant,
touching gently my path, your tones are something

while massaging me lightly, helps me to compose. Standing behind me I am beside myself, your musical scale motivation for me, help me play, keep on touching me always so dear to me. My dear darling I love you a lot'

The keys played so beautifully, how I wish I could play; the notes connected caused emotions to come up every day and evening playing. The combination of the hammers on the strings, the way your voice be singing, you swinging ever so gracefully in your seat. Eyes closed speaking to me with tone.

It has been too long since way back when I would sit close to you to stimulate inspiration. The music sounds the same as I sit here in the room the piano in its original place, listening on the recorder, 'You Are Something Else' a classical composition in A, sitting at the bay bringing back your display for me.

I am having a memory of one of our dates before we vowed to each other, you brought along flowers you chose to arrange for me, I made a sweet grass candle for you. There was an area close by to where you lived, where we often walked and sat and ate...talked of the work ahead back then. Your intelligence and your knowledge of it helped mine to prosper, prosperous believing from the moment we started spending time together, speaking of what we were later able to achieve.

It was so much to look at you through the days, kissing every evening good day, greeting the mornings the same. We both brought along a picnic, sitting up strong, pressed cozy to the grass; our dates lasted as long as the days did, as long as the evenings permitted, kept up thoroughly each time we met. Went on back to places that relaxed our minds to where we could move together as one.

Time passing by, watching the darkness come, holding one another close, keeping us warm on any day since the beginning we dated, kept our love the same, just matured as the days past. Now I sit here on the grass, my mind fixated on nothing in particular, piecemeal you come back to me.

You said to me, 'let us work together, I am inviting you to walk this path with me, I will sing everyday to you, a kiss for you throughout the day all days, I will do. I promise the love will not change but grow, I have already shown growth since meeting you that night; it was for one reason. I will keep that reason at the forefront of my mind to keep us together, I love you right now forever and will never let that subside. Be beside me let us love life together, I will do' and I did too.

Three o'clock in the morning waking up to you, my mind is thinking, my body hot, it has been so long without you. Three o'clock in the morning your spirit speaks to me, guides my soul through my dreams, the dreams we had as one, the feelings we gave our word to, you promised to be with me forever and you are.

There is no end to the spirit you left lingering around, things come up so often through my days that wake me up to the fact that you are gone. I love that we were able to love enough for so long that when you said you

would always be around you meant it. Reassured me
enough with your music that you left me, sang to me, I
continue to hear while I sleep, riding horse drawn
carriage for my birth day not today...my song from you
replayed in my dream last night as I drifted back to a
real day spent with you, singing the song you wrote for
me last night for my birthday at the piano in my dreams;
how I wish I could play!

Merry,
merry of your start
I could feel your heart
from the moment I met you.
Love
I am so happy you were born
A life without you
I could not imagine.
You do more than inspire us...
we have yet to create the word
to express precisely what you do,
who you are,
where you came from,
and how.
It is more than motivation
that moves us with you,
the word not beauty, although
it accurately describes you...
a Gracious Spirit on land
merry of your birth,
you are one of few
who stood tall from the beginning
next to yourself,
surrounded yourself to be able
and worked yourself,

you especially helped me,
but especially the world.
You are essential to our existence
I hope you know
how much the world has grown
because of you.
You have done so much for our spirit, merry of your
start,
so pleased you were born today
Happy birthday to you
Merry of your start to you.

There was consistent wondering about, the way we
caused one another to feel, that is why we both found it
difficult to look at one another from the beginning to the
end. I find it difficult sometimes now to look at your
pictures when I pass them by; there is always depth
showing, love glowing straight to your soul. Exposed
from the beginning for me, it is different seeing what I
seen while you were here with me, now it feels too real
sometimes. Sometimes it feels as if the pictures have
come alive and you are moving about as if you are right
here, or I am there with you. One more moment with
you so wanted I drift into the memories until we are
back together, just when I am missing you as much as I
am right now you lift me up. I do not recall us ever
talking about what it would be like if one of us were not
around, we thought we would be to the end, so we did
everything we could, and should have to keep us
focused on our path.

Gave gifts that have lasted, love everlasting just as we
knew, even if you are not physically here with me, I can
feel you next to me at all times.

I want to go to bed where you are, I want to gaze again with you at the planets and stars, celebrate more holidays and our work with gifts, and end more nights with kisses on your lips. Your favors on me as tokens of your love I sat back and accepted you fully, you relaxed and did not worry as I opened you up further as the years went by. I never expected you to die; so many mornings have gone by, afternoons a lot of loneliness has been around as they past so quickly. The nights have certainly been most lonesome especially this winter; the storms turned all the lights off more often than before. The fire we would have enjoyed together, candles just about every night, drinking hot cider listening to music while waiting for what to write...playing for me while I write.

These nights have had me up inspired again by what successive evenings up have to bring, it is a few days before spring begins. The racks have finally settled together they have been rolling by for days, faint bows of light penetrating through the fog this evening with not much else visible around.

In triple time together we moved through life, you were as special to me as I was precious to you, our similar views and tastes kept cravings new, celebrated time and again to keep the mood as we said we would. Even when there was not much to see on days or some nights, we found ways to penetrate the darkness to find our way closer to one another. To pass greatness down to next generations is what we aspired to do, words and with music, all around care of the land to this day today. Our handle for each other lit the spark to force the journey that which we ensured would be everlasting, joining new connections to our path, adding new benefactors to the theater. So old now. Life together we knew would be transcendent, recalling back all that made life more than enough to write on you, on me and all others too.

I miss you the way I do and all the time will, everything reminds me of you. I went back through the trail and found another spot where I could sit and talk to you, while writing on you.

I held you in my arms last night in my dreams, it was like holding you in the past, our hug continues to feel the same, caresses like from before, while uttering the other's name.

Thank you for those times shared, all the time in high spirits to be with each other, to guide one another on the same path. I want to thank you for keeping your words with me, you said and did what you knew was possible all along, thank you for the songs, the recipes, the mornings and evenings with assurance that matched the quality of mine. For loving me so long to be of the longest to last, a particular life I continue to be a part of while remembering having the characteristics of you close at hand. My hand in my own each evening as I give thanks to the fine day had, my nighttimes held with you in my arms keeps peace in place to keep me going from since the moment you left.

I held you in my arms last night your hands still feel over my back, a warm circular movement felt around my shoulders, around my blades and grasping my waist...keeping my spine straight. To this day this morning I know I have said all along, how I feel you next to me at all times; at times time seems to go back, or I feel as if I am losing it somehow. You smell so close to me, I reach out and when I go back I still feel thou, coming back to real time now wondering where you have gone. I have been living with insomnia once again inspired by what we use to do to keep the other going, nights up writing music to the other, expressing true love I still feel it.

Up all night writing for days; what our souls desired our hearts desired more, our souls knew from before; anxious for our hearts to catch up and before too long they did. We moved with the same pace from the start to the last day I held you in my arms, our hearts by then full to the life our souls promised and brought.

Spring is again here and you can tell by how much it has been raining, time sprung ahead to give us longer evenings; the days long light. Even with all this raining the sun has the clouds a light grey, keeping it lighter than what the winter brought, helping the summer to grow.

It is now preparation for what the summer will be, using my own brightness to get by, and your light-hearted styled memories satisfying me. Enjoying the rain until the sun come back around; splashing in the puddles that I come to as I walk about, getting muddy; brings me back to the memories I vow to never let them go. The fun we had in the rain, we would enjoy all these days and nights together in the rain during this spring. Tangerine therapy always refreshed and energized,

plunged in the bath afterwards drinking down hot
chocolate or cider, sometimes wine or champagne;
depending on the nature of the celebration, we raised
our glasses to the occasion daily merry of our start.

We were thankful for life and what we were given,
our souls giving us direction as we enhanced our path,
the one we came together on. I am wrapped with the
time we used to grow; I do not think there is a thing I do
not know about you and you of me. Your favorite color
green, this particular time during spring got you excited
for what the colors for summer would be. So many
shades of green dominant to the vast colors around, the
rain of spring help your favorite color show, made lush
the field.

You looked splendid sitting on the green under the
tree we planted painting the view, getting ready for
what to compose. It was especially nice watching you
under the umbrella in the rain under the tree when the
blossoms were showing.

I remember painting that...

It is almost a black and white picture, the sky a low
mixture of the two, it is pouring out that afternoon, the
dark green umbrella sheltering you as you paint on the
small canvas on the low level easel. The fog surrounding
makes it look quite mystical as the light from the day
pushes through it, with flowers that come back that time
budding too.
I was under my own canopy painting you, the lake
cannot be seen, nor can the theater across the way; the
paint brush is what stands out with your bracelet

gracing your hand, the canvas and brush color the same, a mug of hot something at hand.

This painting hanging once again now that spring is here, looking out the window sitting on the bay looks similar to that day the painting was a real moment I relive each time it is time to bring it out again. Named it, 'The First Spring' marked on the back the very first painting I ever did of you in spring so long ago; hanging up for spring is here.

These birds come back every seven years, filling the tree and eating all the seeds, they do not seem to like the apple, but they sure do like the cherry. The music they make is incredible; you can tell the babies from the full grown, the males and the females' tones vary, can also tell by the time of day which ones are around. The babies and females like to play around the tree as the males look for what is good for shelter, I entice them with a seed selection and a bath of water they frolic about in; the babies find their way there.

I am not sure of the pattern they follow to find their way back, I just know they have to be the ones that have been coming around since we were here. New ones when they arrive, the matured ones guiding the way, staying as long as spring stays every seven years I awake to the sounds of the music from this group of small birds.

Stretching slowly to the sounds of the music playing I take full advantage as early as they rise I rise too; just as we would do, starting the day off with the eager calls the new births brought back. You are needed now as I am as this season is enthusiastic to creation, creativity, all things new but as they were before, but just with you gone.

With you gone everything reminds me of you, doing everything together and all, capturing at the same time what each of the seasons brought for us, and it brought the same meaning to us if not similar. Like the mirror to the other reflecting our souls contentment; every time I look at something, anything, I am for at least an instant fixated on you with it. Outside under the tree painting me. I cannot look outside without being reminded of you somehow, especially now that it is spring and I have the paintings out once again. You were painting me under the shelter , while you were being captured by me; unbeknownst to me until you came running through the rain with the canvas in your hand...you know I had to take a photograph of that (I will describe it more later)

Your umbrella down, you came under the shelter with me, 'look what I painted' I had a feeling you would be up here capturing the first day of spring here together, I could feel you studying me, and if when I looked close enough I could see that you were gazing upon me. Well this is you, standing here covered from the rain capturing your love, well you are mine, on the back of this first spring together I sign my name and date and promise more to keep, I hope you write on back yours the same I know it is true. I love you and vow more springtime to come around with the excitement the same.

With all that is around and the excitement being the same there is not a day that goes by without thinking about you, I enjoy calling back specific moments spent in the dark whether outside or in, especially in front of the fire cozy together. I light it and enjoy it even if I become sadden by feelings wanted, I smile because of the memories that were had there take me back so long ago.

It has been so long ago, since I held you in my arms in front of the fire in the blanket I made for us, yet the flame burns the same to light the paintings that grace the mantel. I do not recall the last day it was for sure, I do remember us sitting quite often you in my arms, keeping you warm, holding both your hands with mine.

The same paintings off center the mantel with candles, sweet grass, and petals scattered, while you were drifting home; holding you close and welcomed spring before your end. It was not really an end but more of a start to something else, you alive in spirit; your spirit lingering the same in my thoughts and my mind, bouncing about the house unchanged. This is why I feel at ease with you gone; regardless of the tears, there will be sorrow with the easiness that I feel living life with you gone. What I am sad by is what lifts me up most meaning you, it is using everything around to get me not only through, but to keep me thriving, my sides alongside yours gracing the land I feel you here as if using our time together still.

We did not make a sound that day until the end of the night, our hearts they spoke alone, our lips and hips with them dancing, brushing by each other to the combined tones. Moaning and soft pampering by the light of the fire, placed upon my face a glow, your air shining, finding my way to you from it. Through the afternoon all the way through the dark you smiled for

me, returned happiness back to you; we did not say a
word until the earliest part of the morning began. Told
one another we loved each other then babbled through
the rest of the night, held each other nigh, caresses from
my shoulder down to my thigh while I held my hand to
your heart. A warm start to our sleep so that pleasant
dreams we would always keep to wake us up in high
spirits.

The sounds through the night reassuring, lifting us up
with the dawn, still babbling on about our closeness
from the day before and evening pouring from the
creation that was the two of us combined. Sublime
really, having to reflect quietly quite often the level in
which we obtained, in the instant we heard the others
name we were acquainted back with our mate. Your
soul mate met mine, waxing philosophical every day we
lived by our philosophy, our behavior the same, practice
the same.

Our principal rule guided by our decent manners;
your manner with me sublime surely; I long for you to
touch me kindly one more long-lasting time. Mine
touching you, all of what I have on you; in no order our
hands would go, fingers walking o'er each other's body
stimulating our souls back to where they were familiar
long before we knew. At ease with it, pleased to the
height of it we grew to that level with time, from the
inside it showed up on our being the beam, beaming
with me. Seemly characteristics of me brought you to
what I have inside, demonstrated daily on the outside is
what kept us together; healed spiritually the grief.

Our beliefs said out loud before we slumber for the

night, something motivational to keep us waking up to the morning pleased the same, at ease from the message the morning brought us up the same. Toasts to each other the same, toasting my body next to your energy we thrived and lived together for as long as we were able to be.

For as long as I was able to I showed you just what you meant to me, I hope you can hear what I am writing now, I still have the habit of speaking aloud as I write. To the music of your tones, my music maker gone, love maker past feelings arise often that bring me back to you. The mood around me similar in that the depth is not as long, tones not as strong with you not breathing next to me, energy bouncing off of mine, hands consistently on mine to keep our bracelets brushing.

Your tones are gone, yet the memories of them bring them back again, raising the level to where it shall be, the deepness penetrating me deeper, taking me to that joined depth to keep me going.

My heart showing as I write about you this spring, so many have come to pass, the memories lasting in all of me, recalling them with the feelings that have stayed with me since realized were true.

Running cross the field in the rain; that picture hangs in the middle window at the bay. It was taken by me the first spring we were outside painting; you were under your umbrella running to me with canvas in your hand, I kept the camera at hand for capturing details such as these ones. The rain coming down, cloudy from the fog, you clicked your heels to the side, happy running to me,

clicked your heels together in appreciation for me. This
picture makes me feel alive, used the rain as much as the
sun to come alive daily; learned to keep warmth through
the cold months. These pictures keep me up, wake me
up in my dreams as they come alive, these memories
captured in black and white turn to color in real time,
just from loving one another back then.

From all the love back then, true feelings spent
showing out loud, demonstrated in our actions and
comments to each other respectful all the time. I sit
outside protected from the showers so heavy at times
they seem to not let up. Wherever they are, I can hear
the birds singing, can still hear them even though I
cannot see them. Their music comes from all direction
as if it penetrates through everything around it, as if it
moves through whatever is in its way. The vocal skill
vibrating off their sound box to keep them singing non-
stop for what seems to be until the dawn is done,
needing no breaths in-between, as it would seem.

Reminding me of thee and thou vocal range, steady
flow, singing as effortlessly as the morning bird does, I
keep your music turned up to as loud as it was when
you were singing about the house. The booming
penetrating evenly to wherever I am creating about the
days ahead, in the kitchen preparing a meal for that
time, in the bath. I particularly enjoy listening to you as
I soak in the bath, candles lit, surrounding the outline
enough to light the pages, incense or sweet grass
burning; laying back comfortable listening to your
range. Going back on bygone times with you bouncing
off the walls into my soul, warming me up as much as

the bath itself does, and my thoughts of course do too.

Whereas there was no fear while you were here there is none today, our love for life kept us at ease on our path. Our excitement and laughter overshadowed that if we were to ever worry, our solace kept us up without faltering in our steps or of our voices. I look to you to keep me up now and you do, all I need to do is look anywhere in any room and I will see you there, sitting in the bath now with you in here.

Listening to your music together, smiling for each other, relaxed enough to feel your energy, I wish I could stay here forever sometimes with you when I know it is time for you to go. Still around me penetrating my soul, not without the image of you across from me, or at my side. Your image subsides and moves into my mind to keep me mindful, through my soul you keep up the soulful inspiring beats to keep my soul full, just as it was all along...
Now that I have spent enough time in the bath to get me sleepy, I move the candles into the bedroom and fill the fireplace with them. I hope I see you again as I drift into deep relaxation, deep breathing, deep thoughts of you and my nightly hopes for, before I sleep.

I wake up to the birds and the sounds from the wind and rain, it is definitely spring, everything is growing lush with color and the apples are just starting. With the hot apple cider and breakfast I pick up and read what is appropriate for this weather, chapter four of 'The Voyage to Wherever I am 'Found'

Chapter Four: Rain for days

The clouds come quickly rolling over as I prepare for obvious rain; I have felt drops already on my face. I guess you're never really ready for what the storms can bring, I just sit with my pen and wait for it to begin. You will never see rain like this unless you chance the open water. You don't think the waves will get any higher 'til they do, keeping your heart rate up, so exciting. Pouring so hard you can't see a thing in front of you, holding on tight in one place in my quarters looking out the window, showing nothing but rain for days.

Seven days now and it has finally ended, the waves now calmer, the sun burning brightly again and I am glad. It has been too many days since I had enough food, drank mostly juice and water...it was too bumpy to even think about cooking; made you too hungry to anyhow, oh yes, and nauseous. I plan to spend today enjoying the sun while it is out, and then the stars while I can see them, don't know when it will storm again or for how long, so I shall eat enough to keep me full for days, and hang my feet down to the water allowing the waves to carry me to wherever it is I should go...

I am going down to the path I created for you in the year before your birthday. I will groom the land for this weather is perfect for conditioning it; planting more seeds to it. I really hope for the pied orchids to grow as I have planted them, in a heart shape next to the gazebo; much like the jasmine we arranged the same way to paint the other in it and for sitting in. I went to it often in summer now as before it was too difficult to come to it, now I will have motivation for visiting it and draw up inspiration from it as we did on your birthday and any other day we came here to visit this spot.

I can certainly feel it, the excitement that spring brings, outside in the rain; I love to see the rain. Feet wet and cooled by the mud, but warm enough to have my boots off, slacks rolled up, my hood up as I think of what next to do. So much to do!
Taking great care of our home as if you were here, the same spirit for what springtime has consistently brought...even if I miss you a lot.

I miss you now, I miss you so much, as such a time with this creation flowing I know you are enjoying it as much, missing me as much, coming down to keep me from falling back too much. At such a moment as now, somehow the mood has changed. I was sitting here ready to go cross the lake to the theater to get the grounds ready to grow; when I suddenly felt my heart pain, or my soul now pangs for you. Why do I miss you so much when I can feel your presence with me at all times, especially when I am sleeping, I am always keeping pleasant moments from our time for that is all we knew. I have never fathomed loneliness and what is meant by it until the day of your departure, and every day since then my heart sometimes knows exactly the meaning. So many times I go back and that keeps me alive to move forward, but it is as if you have not left while I am recalling. And sometimes not even when I am back in real time do I realize you are gone. It usually becomes painful when I reach my arms out to hold you even closer that I am really without you, but your energy fills the space between where I kept you tight to keep us moving. Even with the sadness there is so much happiness to be had, to hold tightly of to the end until I will be able to say to your face again everything that makes you wonderful.

Every detail that makes you wonderful goes right to the inner most part of you, so much of it, it exudes inside your body and out around it. Your colors so clearly inviting, all the time I see/n them, graceful on your feet you walked about in a confident way to get us to the path and kept us on it. On your words and your melody I will still rave about always, dance about to on special days in the theater and at home, still touching me from afar.

Moving me from a far off place. My eyes throbbing from the tears that cause me to close them to see better, the tingling turns into stars from where I know you must be. Coming down to play with me and as fore, play the games were fun, taunting one another for fun to keep us in the mood.

You were the one I always knew that before I could say it, had the heart to express it, what was in my mind I knew I meant it, what you displayed in return showed it. We showered one another to exemplify our meaning, true to the life we wanted long prior to when met. My eyes wet now with contentment, wanting to pack up to come to you. I am so much older now and satisfied with my life I made the best of it, could not have imagined a better lover, friends to have around, all those we caught up to, brought up. We gathered so much from what we had around us, made a great deal in what we were given to be able to give back....sitting back now reflecting as I have been doing all along.

The apples on the tree have grown to their best size, an abundant of them I gather in a basket recalling you back here doing the same. That is the painting of all of us that is up during summertime. The one I painted after it was photographed of all of us. We had so many recipes that went well with our apples. I will be having friends over after to welcome summer's first night. The apples of course will be for the cold cider to cool us from the heat; and spiced apple cookies...it is almost too hot to eat. Tonight we will keep it simple but satisfyingly filling, our friends will bring ice cream, chocolate and other fruit...will go perfect with the fire. And wine for toasting again by the fire.

I thought it would be fitting to use the spot that I created for us to enjoy in particular on your birthday, to gather our friends around, sit in the middle of the orchids now in full bloom and bring out the paints. One canvas with enough brushes for all to keep at hand for when the creativity starts flowing.

Our matured hearts flowing as I write while inspired by the others, adding my mark to the painting as I am inspired too often. I started with my handprint, following the others before me, and sat to come up with what to turn it into. I was thinking that my palm can be my heart, so therefore I sectioned it off in red; the lines matching those in my heart reflect my palm. My fingers curled protecting over it to keep it pumping, my hand on my own heart is something I always felt it there, it was not until the painting was completed that I realized what I felt all along. Like a hand on my heart keeping me safe to what I aspire to become and therefore did; burning heartfelt in the centers of where all the lines meet together. Our friends' depiction similar in that their hands represent their heart, their fingers protecting some hearts, others giving blessing with different fingers overlapping. Lapping this moment together with the canvas expressing with written words the meaning makes us all cry. Our meaning come to realize all at once within this painting we thought we knew all along.

We come together and we figure something new that causes us to have conversations the night away, all of us giving meaning to each other each time we get to gather around the campfire, or at any time we sit in a circle...tonight, just like all the other days and nights...uplifting.

It must be because our spirits are much closer to the two of you gone together again. Each time we come together the toasts move us along; we all have something to add before the night ends. It usually ends late, not because we cannot find the words to motivate each other, but because we have real motives that lovingly play out, inducing our inner most truths every time to keep us to the next time we come together. I am excited to have the painting here, I will be enjoying it come the first of winter to the first of spring comes back. For now I keep the feeling that erupted from the depth in all of us in the forefront of my mind, the combined meaning of us at hand here in the verse about it I created.

Our hearts on fire,
protection for all
the two of your spirits a swirl around
with extended colors running off.
The colors blend precisely to our meaning,
our lines connecting each other

to our divine unity.

We did not know of this until the painting revealed it.
I mean, we always connected our hands and our arms
when we come to meet, when saying good-bye for now.
Connected our bracelets as we raised the other hand
with our glasses, the one we all received from you one
winter, and have kept them on since then. We all vowed
with rings for our wrists, which kept us connected as we
sat in a circle, if the conversation had our hands
connected...or at some point we made a point of it.

I will start planning tomorrow for your birthday even
though it is a few months away; we are planning to go
away. I think I will plan for us to travel by boat to the
island not too far from here, or maybe venture much
further; they have left the destination up to me.

Destination! To the island nearby, we have not gone
on a boat ride together in a long time, aside from
paddling on the lake. Toasting and eating cake all the
way there, taking long enough to arrive for us to relax
on the waves. Of course we are eating chocolate dipped
fruit, it is tradition, as is the poem I write each year to
read aloud to you this year I will read the same, out loud
to our friends I hope you hear it. Smoothly flowing over
the water I get in my groove to get going, writing your
poem now with inspiration from all that surrounds me.
Our friends, anxious as I am to arrive to celebrate. Some
instruments ready, beating on them feeling the
movement already, almost there.

Happy birthday darling...
we have arrived on the island,

I have decided
to take time out now to reflect on you,
happy birthday to you.
You know I long for you to be here
at this time
at such a time as now so special,
toasting to your birth with champagne...
'here, here'
Our friends have the beat going
I move to it as I am writing,
so happy you were born today
and more so that I met you,
I love you...
I miss you...
I will celebrate you the way we did when you were here,
I toast to your birthday darling
here, here

   The energy from past visits seems fresh on the
ground, the memories here back around as we too sat on
the highest peak. That is one of the images I wanted to
have here, as we are happy for your beginning, and your
soul singing in high spirits. Your energy and your
positive use of it, the path we stayed on together, and
your fingers control over every key.

Happy birthday to all that is thee...
shakers shaking circling me,
to the beat we heard your heart moving to
we move to you now,
happy day to the day you were born
today with us now we celebrate,
happy birthday today.

We had a camp out, just one night; we went back to the sun rising since we stayed up all night. The ride back over was just as nice as getting there, the perfection of the morning combined with friends and already looking back on the hours before. We were such good friends; the laughter from the fun of us is always enjoyable, memorable enough to call on exactly later, chuckle out loud to later. Our hands interlocked with hugs that followed is more than enough to keep me writing, on all that inspired us and continues to.

The perfection of the summertime has kept me in great spirits; the sun has been out now for as long as it was raining, since a few days before the first of summer. This type of weather keeps me out as much as autumn does, and as much as spring does if it is not raining too much. As such temperature as it is these days, I surely am inspired, a continuation of what the spring brought with more motivation from inside. On a peaceful ride on the lake, bouncing on the same spot the hours passing. The heat will obvious be of lasting quality, I can feel it in the air in that there is none at all, the boat moving only with me when I do. It is too hot to. I sit laid back glasses and sunhat on, moving only to get another cup of apple ice, the same hand moving across the pages writing of calm.

I feel that now, undisturbed by the feelings running out across the page, just from keeping what we did all along, believing in me to keep me strong. It does not feel that long ago since I held you last, although if I calculate the time it is so, so I have not ever counted the days down since you left us. Anyway you come when I need you now, I feel you now; you are the only air that is flowing around me now, well besides my own. I can feel it getting warmer the longer I sit and think of you, my hands burning in the center as they always do; when I feel close to you; when I do the work we always did, when I listen to the music you wrote; and when I fall asleep and awake the same the next morning, there is heat on my palms too.

Our treasure was of high value; I sit here and marvel at the thickness of the blades, the deep color of them blending with every flower has blossomed. The constant showers from when spring was here have certainly enhanced the summer; it always does. But this particular summer for me stands out, looking forward to tomorrow, contented by your visits you come back to me daily. Or at least by night-time I feel you around, the sounds here on the lake rocking ever so gently from side-to-side, to the movement I now am feeling tonight. Encompassed with your temperament rising or maybe it is mine rising to you. What my body goes through feels similar to when you were sitting across from me in the boat, laughing and joking, toasting flowers we brought along to the water. We loved each other more as the days past used our surroundings to get by; our energy causing our glow to be revealed, feelings real to where we knew possibilities could go.

And they went, and they are endless in that we continue to do as we are supposed. I sit and add to the theater still this year. Preparing for another act to my play. It is still to this day gathering the pain and discarding it away, healing spiritually through our prayers on each other, wishing peace, love and family for all. Acting of what we saw together on lands similar to the one in which we made our home, making things better today, taking firm hold of each other's hands whenever we can. Calling out for each other as we end the night, the same as tonight as I sleep now from the entire day spent into the evening on the lake.

In the middle of the water between the theater and our home, my dream continued on that spot. Back relaxing there I hear more clearly the calls of the birds wherever they may be, their echoes surround me in beautiful colors, the most vibrant of ultramarine. There are two yellow swirls in the center, one a few shades lighter moving in opposite directions, the water clear enough to see the bottom as I am fascinated by the number of sand dollars on the bottom. Their deep maroon color goes nicely with the clear light blue water.

I begin to paddle to the side where the theatre is, just at this time it is not created yet, my younger days. I can see it in my face, the color of my hair unchanged from time, not too much has gone by; I think I knew you then in my dreams, I could feel you there with me even though I could not see you anywhere.
(You came by to see me in my next dream; I have already written it to recall it later)
I sat at the spot where the theatre would later be, I felt you. I could hear you speaking to me as I seem to be pleading, calling out for what was all I needed. You, work and everything else that combined to create exactly all I wanted, the celebrations with the lot around us, taking away and left things on lands we visited as often as we could and should have.

Invited far off friends to come back, taught them

things to take back, songs and food prepared together to enhance the flavors of us combined. The truth of the plays, poetry, music and artwork, with the fulfillment of the food, set us static stature in the mood to keep the healing going.

Act one scene four is coming up now, we show the connection we have in our pain and of our desires, what we aspire to feel is the same. We need family and friends of exceptional quality to help us develop, we need to keep the land up; grow stuff, do exactly what we have been known to. Food and water plentiful enough, soul mates to all with one in particular to sleep next to, to wake to, and be moved by to keep moving, take careful time...if you desire one to.

Past pain keeping us humble, 'don't wanna go back there no more', this lifestyle worth holding on strong to stay lasting, handing on what we aspired to do.

That is what I meant when I said I am ready to pack it in to come to you, I am pleased with and have been relaxed with all we did and continue to do. I miss you. It has been a long time I know I still cry for you, a natural reaction after reaching out to you to find you unreachable. Acting feelings from in my dreams gets the flow coming, tingling stars first appear, eyes closed to the throbbing in the center of me. To the tips of my hands and feet that tingles my fingers and my toes, I wish I had you here to walk my fingers around, fiddle my toes with yours and up and down each other's calf. Getting your goose pimples rising, raising mine all over me, letting go easily as if you are here, the memories clear enough to this evening to cause you to come back to me.

Thinking of thoughts just to write about you...walking around twisting our shoulders to each other. Your piano music went well in the theater to get us started, continued through the motion of my plays; up moving our shoulders swaying to the key players, drummers, and bell shakers through the evening, the harpsichord masters and harmonica jammers.

We handclap for rhythm and our handclasps firm to each other; we understand the meaning of our birth and continue to work toward completeness, speaking of you quite often rejoicing your spirit. The theater has been filled with music, the perfection of this summer has been especially inspiring to us all, we are together calm in our feelings, our dealings as one in a kind-hearted way, openly displaying our higher meaning, our morals and values much the same, value all the same, quality leveling to our propriety, discarding all the pain and hurt the plays made from real.

Act one, scene three
Young Latoya sits in the center of the stage swaying to the piano looking up at the audience...she begins...

I will be great, my grandparents always praised me before they died, told me my name means exactly how they talk to me. Now I am happy I get to go to school each day, my teachers look at me the same way they did. It doesn't matter I am hiding my pain, I hate my home, my neighborhood makes me afraid to go out, but I go to school and work to get food, medicine, water plentiful enough to keep us going. I take care of everything since my father is gone, my mother's mind is gone, health gone too...too many siblings to look after, but every day

I do. I get up and go to school, and work for food,
taking on that mother role, I am the oldest not old
enough, but regardless of my situation at home I get up
and push on...my Grandparents praised to me, 'you
special my girl'

Spotlight fades from Latoya while focusing on a
young Wuti sitting to the left of the stage, moving to the
piano playing she begins.

I know why they are enraged so that is why I choose
to stay away from it; I am not that young to have a
problem with it, most everyone else around me does.
They take it out on me especially because they don't like
me, they always tell me that, and slap me around for
being here. I read all the time to get away, wishing if
only I could be one of the characters I read about, so I
hope for a better life to come true. I was told by my
elders early on to stay in school, but they won't let me
go, therefore I learn on my own. When they sleep I take
time to learn what they won't teach me, but how can I
succeed with nobody next to me, locked in my home
afraid to speak of what we need...I Look in the mirror
when they pass out and repeat what my elders praised
in me.

Spotlight moves from Wuti and focuses on Eileen who
is swaying while sitting to the right on the stage...she
begins.

I don't think it's right keeping me here even though
they say it will be fine, they have been saying that since I
was five, I should have told my mother before she died.
Now it is just one guardian with the four of us girls, it

hasn't been easy trying to keep hands off them. I am the oldest here to protect, needing it from myself, I sit here hurting myself for what has been done. I don't want to do it, but maybe I think I am bad, but I know it's not my fault, I come back home because I have to come in. I have the girls to think about, the prayers to my mother will work if I keep talking to her, I can't go through any more of this being done, how long does it hurt, how long does pain last...

All three girls remain sitting on the stage, sitting together in a triangle holding hands...

Alternating every two lines Eileen begins, then Wuti then Latoya in that order,
I AM BEAUTIFUL
I will no longer believe you as I have before
I AM DESERVING
what you said doesn't matter to me anymore
I AM STRONG
you will no longer bring me down,
I WILL HEAL
because of the greatness in me I found,
I WILL SUCCEED
at what I want that is best for me
I AM ELATED
because of all the fine things in me I see,
I AM OUTSTANDING
it shows in everything I have done
I DO BELIEVE
in me, this means I've won
I AM INTELLIGENT
because of what I was taught to believe
I AM WONDERFUL

it doesn't matter to me what you see
I AM LOVABLE
I don't need to hear that from you
MY FEELINGS COUNT
along with everything else I go through
(all together)
I AM BEAUTIFUL, I AM ELATED, I AM
INTELLIGENT,
I AM DESERVING, I AM LOVABLE, I AM
WONDERFUL,
I WILL SUCCEED, I AM OUTSTANDING, I DO
BELIEVE,
MY FEELINGS COUNT AND I AM STRONG,
all the things I allowed you to put in my head
were so very wrong....I AM STRONG!

The celebration last night has just ended, started in the afternoon with friends getting ready at home, then early to the theater. Back across the lake and celebrated more on the field, slept out there, just getting in now.

As it normally is the crowd met hand-to-hand, danced to the music after the plays, using your music within the rest as we repeatedly did. Our music maker gone, but we still use the recordings you left for us to play with the performances, all the others to continue us dancing while the others break to greet. Kept to our feet from the moment we begun, I mean from the afternoon with friends we were standing until now, I still have it in me even with all the years that have past. The excitement and talent keeps us up to the occasion, oblivious to the time passing, using our time together to grow.

There will be another week in-between before we have the celebration at the end of the month for all who have birthdays this month to come to, others welcomed to join too.

We make enough apple-baked cakes and apple pies to feed all we know will come, starting tomorrow with the preparations. Enough food to last the night out, toasting with orange-champagne drink, and wine, ringing in 'til next morning together. We toasted happy birthday to all, starting from those born on the first, which is why these celebrations will always last longer than a day.

There will be thirty-one toasts this month taking place each hour, open-stage entertainment and every instrument we use will outline the stage, two pianos interlocked on the stage. We have anyone who would like to toast come up in natural flow, one after another the inspiration flows, happy for each birth. We toast each hour and play music around as we speak, we eat, we light a candle that burns throughout the night for all whose day it is to wish on, and when it goes out that is when we toast one last time to welcome next month's birth.

I am contented from last night, tired but alive, I will spend the next days starting today putting together a recipe book to leave with all the recipes promised.

**Inspiration from the
apple tree we planted**.

Introduction:

Many years ago I recall us planting a tree we would use year round, naturally we decided on apple since we enjoyed them so much, and had so many recipes added to the ones handed down.

There is a little more to planting an apple tree than this, this is most of it, you will have to do a bit of research on it...the more you read about it, the stronger your tree will be and therefore the apples will be their best too.

There is not really that much work to do...

Sometime during the beginning of spring dig a hole where the tree will see the sun at least six hours of the day. Make that hole two feet wider than the roots of the tree. After planting the tree place a cloth around the trunk for protection from outside animals. You will need to place a symmetrical stake beside it for support for the rest of the tree's life; be sure to bind it with protected wire. Fertilization takes place the first month after planting and then again the year after to the day; its birthday if I may.

As exciting as it will be to see the apples on the tree after only two years of growing, there is still a little more work that needs to be tended to before they will be at their strongest. You must pick all the apples off on its second birthday, to develop strength for later years. Year three you will be able to leave some of the apples on the tree, leaving the largest one on the leader branches. Now you will thin the apples on the tree for the first seven days of June, removing three quarters of them; this will develop large apples and good buds for the next years.

   There you have it, an apple tree that will last you twenty-five years.

Apple Canning and Apple Freezing
Wash and peel and core apples. Cut apples into bite-size pieces and boil three to five minutes in thinner syrup (cuppa sugar, 3 cups of water, boil together until the sugar is dissolved) Pack nicely in jars leaving a half-inch from the top, fill with boiling syrup. Tightly close lids and proceed processing in boiling water bath; quart jars = 25 minutes, pint jars = 20 minutes.

Freezing Apples

Wash, peel, core and slice apples (prevent discoloration) Blanch 2 minutes in boiling water or slice apples into chilled syrup.

Table of contents
1. Spiced Apple Cider
2. Apple Jelly
3. Salmon with Apple Jelly
4. Apple Pie
5. Apples and Sweet Potatoes
6. Chicken Breasts Fillets with apples, mustard
and cream
7. Apple Spinach Salad with Blue Cheese Dressing
8. Apple Bake Cake
9. Apple bread
10. Curried Apple Soup
11. Curried Apple Butter with Halibut
12. Apples with other Fruit for Chocolate and Caramel
Fondue
13. Apple Pancakes Baked, with spiced yogurt and cider
syrup
14. Apple Ice
15. Candy Apples, Caramel and Taffy
16. Apple Cider over Homemade Ice Cream
17. Homemade Ice Cream
18. Apple Cider Baked Beans
19. Apple and Pumpkin Pie
20. Apple Chicken Salad
21. Apple Cheese
22. Apple Chutney
23. Applesauce Cookies
24. Apple Sauce
25.Home made butter
26.Turkey with gravy
27. Apple Butter Pumpkin Pie

Spiced Apple Cider

Two gallon of homemade apple cider, two cups of brown sugar, eight cinnamon sticks halved, two tablespoons of allspice and cloves.
Using a string, tie cinnamon, allspice, and cloves in a coffee filter. Mix cider and brown sugar in a pot...add the coffee filter filled with spices, bring to a slower boil. Turn heat to low and simmer ten to fifteen minutes.
*Cider can be kept hot in a slow cooker on low

Apple Jelly

4 kg of our apples and 4 liters of water, the rinds from 2 thinly pared lemons, sugar (about 800 grams for liter of cooked extract) Wash and cut apples using every part of it, add the lemon and simmer for an hour and a bit until apples tender. Test for the pectin level, if good; allow to it to drip for an hour in a scalded jelly bag...then put it in the cleaned pan and heat it. Weigh it and add the appropriate amount of sugar, stir until well dissolved...bring to a gentle boil and make sure it is set then remove from heat, add to sterilized jars, they will keep for a year in your pantry.

Salmon with Apple Jelly

Two teaspoons finely snipped fresh thyme
One teaspoon finely snipped fresh rosemary
Two teaspoons dried juniper berries, crushed
cup dry Vermouth
cup apple jelly (homemade)
Salmon fillets
freshly ground black pepper
extra rosemary, and thyme to garnish
homemade bread

Toast the juniper until fragrance, boil the Vermouth to toast the berries, add in much of the rosemary and thyme, simmer in the apple jelly, heat one minute then set aside. Preheat oven 400 degrees while in a skillet brown salmon backside up first then front then add to an ovenproof pan. Spoon glaze carefully over each fillet, sprinkle garnish smoothly over each fillet, serve with rice, fresh vegetables, homemade bread, candles, a large bouquet and champagne.

Apple Pie

12 of our cooking apples
1 1/2 cups of sugar
4 tablespoons of fresh lemon juice
 6 tablespoons of cinnamon and of cornstarch
1/2 teaspoon of nutmeg
6 tablespoons of butter and a dash of salt.
Core, peel and slice the apples; add the lemon juice and
mix well. Mix some of the cinnamon and sugar together
and add to the bottom of the crusts, and add one
tablespoon of cornstarch to both. Divide apples in half
and split them between the crusts (a quarter on each
shell) Sprinkle half if the cinnamon, sugar, nutmeg and
one tablespoon of cornstarch for each (a quarter for
both) then add a quarter of the remaining apples to the
crust, then the other. Add cinnamon, sugar, nutmeg and
cornstarch...ingredients will fill high! Divide three
tablespoons of butter evenly in dots over each pie, top
with a second crust and cut off any extra, seal and
ventilate.

Apples with Sweet Potato

Apples with one-pound sweet potato, home-
grown, peeled the apples cored. One half a cup apple
cider, homemade, one-third cup dried cranberries, same
made. Boil the sweet potatoes in a basket over water; let
them steam ten minutes 'til tender.
Add other three ingredients to another pan, cover and
cook five minutes or until apples soften. When the sweet
potatoes are done drain off and gently stir in the apple
cider mixture, cook over low heat 'til flavors combine.

Chicken Breasts Fillets with Apples, Mustard and Cream

One tablespoon plus one tea of vegetable oil, six boneless skinless, chicken breast fillets. Three large apples, home-grown cooked and cored, a cup of cider, homemade, one table plus one-teaspoon stone ground mustard, two-thirds a cup and add two tablespoons of cream.

Heat oil in pan over medium heat, add chicken and cook thoroughly, remove from heat, but keep it warm. Add apple slices cook three minutes, add the cider, mustard and cream, boil it together and reduce by three. Spoon apples and cream over chicken.

Apple Spinach Salad with homemade Blue Cheese Dressing

2 cloves of minced garlic
4 tablespoons of red wine vinegar
4 tablespoons of good quality olive oil
2 teaspoons of Worcestershire sauce
just about 2 pounds of spinach, washed, no stems in big enough pieces
4 apples, cubed and no seeds
1/2 pound of crumbled blue cheese
2 cups homemade croutons
Combine first 4 ingredients in a jar with a tight fitting lid, shake, shake, shake it.
Combine spinach, apples and cheese in a bowl, pour dressing over; add freshly ground black pepper and croutons...toss and enjoy.

Homemade croutons

Brush day old homemade French bread and rye bread with olive oil, slice garlic cloves in half and rub over both sides of bread. Cut into crouton size pieces and bake in oven, or pan fry until croutons are achieved, can add fresh herbs after to these.

Apple Bake Cake

Four of our apples peeled, cored, and sliced, ½ cup firmly packed brown sugar, cup and 3 tablespoons all purpose flour, 1/4 teaspoon ground cinnamon, tablespoon orange juice, 2 teaspoons lemon juice both freshly squeezed, teaspoons orange zest, 3 tablespoons chilled, unsalted butter, and 1/4 cup of chopped pecans. Preheat oven to 375 degrees F.

Combine
Apples, 1/2 of the brown sugar, 1-tablespoon flour, and cinnamon in a bowl. Combine orange juice and zest in another bowl and then drizzle in previous bowl. Combine rest of the flour and sugar in a mixing bowl. Cut butter in until mixture looks like course meal.
Stir in pecans and sprinkle mix over the apples and bake until top is brown and apples tender...about 2400 minutes.

Apple Bread

Four cups of flour, one tablespoon of baking soda, half a teaspoon nutmeg, one and a half teaspoons of cinnamon, and a quarter tea of salt...combine all and set aside. Five eggs, one teaspoon of vanilla, two cups of sugar, half cup of homemade applesauce, one cup of brown sugar and one cup of oil...beat well and add to dry mixture, mix well. Bake at 350 degrees 'til done.

Curried Apple Soup

Four teaspoons of oil, a half cup each of diced onion, celery and carrots...home-grown. Four apples, three teaspoons of curry powder, a half cup of flour, ten cups of homemade chicken broth, two cups of drained canned tomatoes, four whole cloves, two teaspoons of parsley minced, two teaspoons of sugar, one teaspoon of mace and freshly ground black pepper and salt.
Heat oil in a large pot over medium heat and add the onion, celery, carrots and apples and sauté for seven minutes. Mix together curry powder with the flour and sprinkle over pot mixture...add chicken broth and cook for four minutes. Then add in the parsley, cloves and tomatoes...then the sugar, mace and salt and pepper. Cook covered twenty-five minutes, discard cloves and serve with homemade bread.

Apple Butter

Combine the following ingredients in a slow cooker and
cook on low for fifteen hours. Then carefully spoon
apple butter into hot jars prepared for jarring then
seal...be sure to the process each pint jar in a pot of
boiling water.
14 cups of homemade applesauce
3 cups of honey
 4 cups of homemade apple cider
2 teaspoons of cinnamon
1 teaspoon allspice
1/2 teaspoon of cloves if you'd like

Halibut with Apple Butter, curried

Half cup of apple butter and mayonnaise, two large
thinly sliced shallots, two slices of crisp bacon,
crumbled; one teaspoon of curry powder and eight
halibut steaks. In a medium bowl combine every
ingredient except for the halibut in a bowl. Line a baking
pan with foil. Mix the ingredients well and then brush
both sides of the Halibut with it and broil five inches
from the heat for ten minutes for each inch of
thickness...goes well with home-grown baked potatoes
and fresh vegetables sautéed in olive oil and garlic.

Apples with other Fruit for Chocolate and Caramel
Fondue

One package of caramel and chocolate chips for every
four of you around the fondue...add another fondue for
each set of four guests.
 While caramels are melting, prepare apples, grapes,
cherries, bananas, and pineapple on a platter. When
caramel is smooth add the chocolate chips and stir with
fondue fork...enjoy

Apple Baked Pancakes

Four large eggs, cuppa milk, one half teaspoon of salt,
two-thirds cup of flour and two tablespoons of sugar.
Six tablespoons of homemade butter, one half-teaspoon
cinnamon, four tablespoons of sugar, two apples
washed, cored, peeled and rings. Beat the eggs until
foamy, beat milk in and add two tablespoons of sugar,
mix the salt and flour together and add in.
Preheat oven to 450 degrees
Next you will need to add the butter to an ovenproof
pan, arrange apples in, a single layer on the pan until
they sizzle. Pour the batter in and make sure it is even;
cover and bake about eight minutes then uncovered for
another eight minutes...remove from oven and sprinkle
with rest of sugar and cinnamon.

Apple Ice

Four and a half pounds of apples, three cups of water,
two and a quarter cups of sugar, one and a half
teaspoons of lemon peel.
Combine the apples, water and sugar in a pot and bring
to a boil, then simmer until the apples soften. Add to
food processor and puree, add in lemon. Pour onto
three nine-inch metal pans and freeze until just firm
enough to remove and add once more to the food
processor until fluffy. Pack in tightly sealed containers
and freeze until needed.

Apple Ice another way

16 apples, 2 lemons, 4 ounces of sugar, 8 tablespoons of
Brandy, 1 pint of whipped double cream, Chocolate
shavings or leaves
Cut the tops off the apples and core them and hollow
out the flesh to use later. Be sure to leave a 1/2 inch shell
and brush the apples with the lemons, then put on tray
and put in the freezer. Cook the chopped apples with
the lemon zest and juice in a pan a 4 tablespoons of
water, cook 'til tender and then add in the sugar and
Brandy, cool down then fold the cream in the now
cooled puree and put into two containers for an hour,
beat mixture then freeze until it is halfway frozen. Add
the mixture to the apples, put apples in a freezer bag and
freeze, remove for one half of an hour, then be sure to
add the chocolate before serving.

Candy Apples, Caramel and Taffy

Caramel Apples

6 packages of caramels equal to 90 ounces, 15 ounces per pack, 12 tablespoons of water, 1/2 teaspoon of salt, 36 wooden skewers, 36 apples, and pecans or peanuts chopped fine.
In a double boiler over simmering water melt caramels, stir until smooth then mix in salt. Put a skewer in each blossomed end of apples. Coat apples with caramel and sprinkle with nuts, place on baking sheets lined with wax paper. Refrigerate until firm.

Taffy Apples

4 cups of sugar
 2 cups of brown sugar
1 1/3 cups each of butter and light corn syrup,
 2 cups of good cream
4 teaspoons of vanilla
2 teaspoon of salt
Put the wooden skewers in the apples, then mix all ingredients in a large pot, cook to 246 degrees while stirring continuously, then remove from heat and allow to thicken. Dip apples quickly in and twist them until they are coated evenly. Place on waxed paper and allow them to firm up, chill in refrigerator if desired.

Homemade Ice Cream

12 beaten eggs, 8 cups of milk, 4 cups plus 12 tablespoons of sugar, 4 cups of half and half cream, 6 cups of whipping cream, 4 tablespoons plus 2 teaspoons of extract vanilla,
1/2 a teaspoon of salt.
Beat eggs and sugar well together, add all other ingredients and mix well, very well. Pour into ice cream freezer cans and leave room at the top to allow for expansion...enough for a 2 gallon freezer...and freeze.

*Can add hot apple cider to it to have apple cider over homemade ice cream.

Apple Cider Baked Beans

Four cups of white navy beans (picked over, discarding broken beans, off colored ones, dirt and rocks if any). Wash beans in four changes of cold water then cover in six inches of water and soak through the night.
2 small onions, finely diced, 8 tablespoons of molasses, 4 teaspoons of black pepper, dried thyme, tomato paste, 2 bay leaves, 8 teaspoons of soy sauce, 2 teaspoons of cider vinegar, 2 2/3 cups of boiling cider, boiling water. Preheat oven 250 degrees. Drain beans but keep the liquid. Bring liquid to boil, add beans to bean pot and add all the ingredients and mix. Add boiling reserve enough to cover the beans, bake 6 hours, adding more water if needed after half time of cooking.

Apple Butter Pumpkin Pie

Two cups of apple jelly and pumpkin
One cup of brown sugar
One quarter teaspoon of ginger
One teaspoon of salt
One and a half teaspoon of cinnamon and nutmeg
Six eggs beaten lightly
Combine all ingredients except eggs in a bowl...add eggs
and mix together well; add milk until it is smooth. Pour
into two pie shells and bake for 40 minutes at 450
degrees.

Apple Chicken Salad

1/4 cup of yoghurt
1/8 cup of orange juice
1/4 cup of apple jelly
1/2 tablespoon of juice from lemon
1 1/2 cups of cooked chicken
1 1/2 cups of diced apples, washed and cored, peel on
1 cup of celery
In a medium sized bowl combine the orange juice,
apple jelly, yoghurt and lemon juice in a bowl. Add
chicken in then the apples and celery are next...toss to
coat nicely together all the ingredients. Chill until the
flavors combine and it is chilled, add on a bed of lettuce,
or on thickly sliced homemade bread, and add sliced
tomatoes, bean sprout, grated cheese and lettuce...will
make 4-6 sandwiches.

Apple Cheese

In a bowl combine one package of cream cheese (at room temperature to be able to work with it better), two tablespoons of juice from a lemon, and one cup of cheddar cheese grated...mix then grate in directly one nice size apple...mix a bit. Add a half a teaspoon of freshly ground black pepper and a teaspoon of either basil or thyme, mix it then refrigerate it.
Serve on crackers or apple slices.

Apple Chutney

Combine the following ingredients in a large pot on medium heat until the sugar dissolves, simmer until mixture thickens. Pour into prepared jars and seal, then process in a ten- minute water boil.
 Ten cups of apples, washed, cored, peeled and chopped, two pounds of brown sugar, two cups of green pepper, one cup of chopped ginger, candied. Two seeded lemons sliced, one half a cup of almonds slivered (if you like) four cups of vinegar, four teaspoon of mustard seeds and 3 teaspoons of salt.

Applesauce Cookies

1/2 cup homemade butter
1 cup honey
3 cups homemade applesauce
2 large eggs
 4 cups whole-wheat pastry flour
2 teaspoons nutmeg and cinnamon
1 teaspoon ground up cloves
2 teaspoons baking powder
1 teaspoon baking soda
1 teaspoon sea salt
2 tablespoons raw sugar
Preheat oven 350* F.

Cream butter and honey well (use a mixer if there is one,
if not cream well) Add applesauce, eggs (one at a time)
and then vanilla; beat well. In another bowl, add flour,
spices, and sea salt, baking and soda powders; mix well.
Add dry to honey mixture, mix well (adding half of the
flour mixture at time)
Drop by teaspoon full on greased cookie sheet and
sprinkle with raw sugar. Bake fifteen-twenty minutes
per batch until lightly brown, cool down on racks, then
package them up. This recipe makes a lot of cookies, so
be sure to give them out.

Apple Sauce

4 1/2 pounds apples, peeled cored and in small wedge
pieces
1 1/3 cup water and sugar and 1 teaspoon cinnamon.
Combine all ingredients in a good pot over
medium/high heat to bring to a boil, then immediately
to low to simmer until apples are very soft...seven to
eleven minutes. If there is a food processor, you can add
apples to it after cooking to puree, if not use whisk to stir
apple sauce while it is cooling to puree by hand.

Homemade Butter

1 pint of good quality heavy cream
Sterilize an airtight glass jar; fill jar halfway with the
cream and place cover securely on. Shake until
thickened...less than twenty minutes, or twenty minutes.
1 pint yields almost 2 1/2 cups

Turkey with Apples

One whole turkey washed and dried and stuffed with
two washed, cored and sliced apples, and salt and
pepper to taste. Pour two cups of the cider in the
roasting pan and roast turkey at 350 degrees, cook it
according to its size. Brush with a tablespoon of butter
and put it back in the oven uncovered until
brown...when it is finished set it aside.
Melt two tablespoons of butter in a pan, and mix in two
tablespoons of flour, and two cups of apple cider. Cook
until it becomes a bit thicker and bubbly then cook just
for another minute...apple gravy for your turkey.

Under the apple tree we replanted every twenty-one years, (this one the fourth) I sit here now and go back more to those times before you were gone. With your songs playing in the background for me as I retrace the path in which we lead, I feel as good as the intentions we pledged to long before the last moment we kept.

It has been so long since the last moment I sat close to your side, looking up at the stars, shoulders to shoulders head on your head on mine. The constellation lines as clear as they were to be on the nights they were given, giving us added consolation, looking up mesmerized.
Thank you for giving me you. Now that summer is through this year and fall is colorfully here, I find myself in high spirits with the season. The summertime had great feeling although you were missed and still are. Looking at the fall stars as clear as it is to have much of them showing tonight, relaxes me to begin the memories of you once again.

On occasions like this one coming, it is still nice celebrating like the way we would, the way we said we should to keep us happy. Thanks for giving me that, it has kept me contented, as content as the smiles that came about when we were living it together...now we celebrate in spirits, still as high as they were, just different now. Thank you somewhat fills what we did for one another, to help with others; it somewhat expresses how I want to tell you how you changed my life forever from the moment I seen you on the stage. Thank you, but with deepness in my voice and through my eyes, with my hands in thine...thank you for you.

Thanks for giving day lasts the month because we
have so much to be thankful 'bout. The theater stays
filled up, cups filled raised up, music up, high spirits
going further, matching the colors of the scene.
To the dreams that were really at hand
the view that which fills us up,
the rhythm fills us up
unified, so we are whole to what we wanted all along
was here at hand. Thankful we knew to come to gather
on occasion to keep us together as one, taking care of all
around, including the grounds.

With the thankfulness tradition beginning anon I
gather words about you that I will read, something I
have done yearly since you were gone to begin this
particular month. A lot of friends remember you
especially during this time, at such a month like this one
coming with you gone are always difficult. To hear the
beautiful words said about and written about you pulls
my heart through the many memories we all have of
when you were here.

I am not the only one who feels your spirit near, there
is hardly a soul who feels you have not left, or at least
you impacted us so much to keep us going. No matter
we all feel you, felt you, remember you the same to keep
us going for as long as the going will be. For as long as
we are going to be we will be alive with your memory,
we vow to keep you in mind specially during thankful
times, but especially to keep us going every day. You
kept your heart showing which kept us open, and now
we keep you in our hearts to keep it pumping, souls
jumping to wherever you be now looking over us.
Your fingers,

and your soul,
up and down up and down the keys
your fingertips,
and your heart,
deciding which way to go
'Romantic Fingers'
the quest for them found, in the instant you walked on
the stage into my life, down and up the keys you kept
me up with thee, right now you do, I can see you for real
and hear you, I feel you. The combination of your mind
and your spirit lingering here, the things we learned
together I will forever use to guide us together again, the
times were too important to do anything else with them
anyhow.

Just as soon as my time ends; I can almost feel it, I am
so old now. Somehow I walk about the same way as I
always have with you and with our friends. Another
one's time has ended. We gave thanks yesterday with
the changed leaves as our background scene, on the field
after the ceremony was held. We held our friends with
high regard; now the three of you are off together, high
somewhere amongst the stars. Calling down for us as
difficult as it is to feel it, we feel each of you gone; I feel
especially you.

I especially feel you as the years pass, as the past
comes up to keep me going, our work going.

Act two scene one:
Serwa, Kimeri, Chunna, Latoya, Wuti and Eileen are all
seated in a circle on the stage; the piano in the
background is cheerfully playing. They have their
hands connected and they are swaying...to the right, to
the left, to the center...center...right, left, center...

Serwa begins:

Thanks for giving me you Kimeri, Chunna, Latoya, Eileen and Wuti, thank you for helping me, showing me that my name is equal to every part of that which is me. For taking my pain from me by sharing yours therefore I am not alone. Serwa Noble woman, thank you for walking with me.

Kimeri:
I'll clap to that, I feel that, I thank you for lifting me up like that, showing my face like that, with smiles and all that comes about through my eyes now that I believe what my name says I am. Thank you Serwa and Chunna, Latoya, Eileen and Wuti, Kimeri a woman, thank you for showing me, me.

Chunna:
And I thank you too, Serwa, Kimeri, Latoya, Eileen, Wuti, for picking me up off the streets, on my feet now so proud to have been born. My friends with the same name you have brought me the joy in which I knew I would bring, would cause someone to sing about, Thank you for showing me that.

Latoya:
My friends you have praised me, raising me as my grandparents have; to the level comfortable enough to rest. The growth of what I wanted to believe all along is intact now, known now in my soul. Our path together has caused me to cry out, shout to the friendship that came about to make me thankful for you Eileen and Wuti and Serwa and Kimeri and Chunna...thank you.

Wuti:
Thank you will start to cover what it means to now feel
me, Eileen, Serwa, Kimeri, Chunna, and Latoya. Thank
you for your hands being raised to hug me a lot, it is
what my soul has needed; I never realized it was all I
lacked...the comfort from soft hands, a warm embrace or
two. Thank you for being in my class to teach me, learn
from me and for showing me my name...Wuti a woman,
thank you for showing me that.

Eileen:
Serwa, Kimeri, Chunna, Latoya, Wuti, thank you for that
and all of this. It does not hurt for long once you are
surrounded with encouragement, believe your name
sent; as you all caused me to believe. Confidence in
myself is all I needed all along, my name highlighted to
lift me along. In this circle now with friends I give great
thanks to you all, stand tall...
Serwa: It does not hurt forever
Kimeri: The pain does end
Chunna: You will be worthy of your birth
Latoya: I am your friend
Wuti: I will be close to you always
Eileen: Our name the same
All: WOMAN, noble, beautiful, strong woman...I'll
handclap for that.

The wind catches my breath as I walked the field and
back, no matter if I turned my back to it, it finds a way to
catch me. I hold my breath and think about you walking
towards wherever we decided to go, missing you so
much as I walk upon the field today, sun as warm as it
can be through the crispness of the fall. I sit under the
tree and I think about the actions in which we grace, to

gather the way we continue to is much like, well what we have known it to be.

   Thinking about thee. I always think about you. You came up over cider yesterday evening as I sat on the same spot, the wind today not as windy as it was last night. I could hardly read aloud as I was writing about you, something I have always done and plan to do until I am done. Writing about someone as special as you, especially since it is you for real, we all feel the same about you as was expressed last night. Honored us again last night for the work we did together and what I continue to do through you. Your music inspired us as it always did, what you prepared for us to keep before you left.

   I can never forget the words we promised to each other, and the reasons our friends celebrate us together, and how we rejoice with them whenever we find special times to get together. I am alive for what we knew was important within the spirit of the world, even though your absence is missed so much. I am selfless enough to know that same love lies within all of us, to keep me alive this long, to write about you and your songs; playing in the background for me on the recorder as I sit up under the tree.

   I believe in you and what you brought to the world, I believe in myself enough to have been joined with you, matched you. My dreams from long ago brought up you before you came round, my spirit found you, or yours found its way to me. In any way you came you came directly at me, what I desired and called out for first came true in my dreams, evidently we knew to come together.

As it is the feast for thanks for giving day tomorrow, I will prepare our traditional dishes while our friends prepare their favorite dishes too. The turkey and apple gravy, I will do, along with the apple butter pumpkin pies, and chocolate and caramel fondues. We will have enough of the regular trimmings and wine to entertain each other until the morning begins and we can start to make the apple pancakes and everything we enjoy added to them.

It is so exciting waiting for our friends to arrive, their drive here must be the same. We are looking forward to having the theater packed again, singing and dancing, my thanks for giving play with your music. I wish you could be here with us. Thank you so much for you. The recipes you left for us to use while we are apart too, for our start being just like our end, for being my best friend is you. Will always be you. Thank you will never cover you, but it will have to do when writing appreciation for you, and everything you have done and continue too. Thank you for our friends that are coming soon and that continue to come around with every season change, holiday, and celebrations like the one coming tomorrow.

So too the tears will not subside, but they are not sad, we are so happy for what we have and have had all along, expressing that daily and through the evenings too. Taking time out to give thanks especially during this time, but especially all the time we can.

I can remember exactly this month long celebration the last one had with you, preparing the same food I will soon do. Sitting with our friends in a circle getting all the vegetables ready, and the outside ready for the day and night. From our field to the theater we filled ourselves up, until the sun came up, the sounds at times too much so it filled our eyes up to start the tears flowing. Not sad, content with knowing, souls showing we are all the same, celebrated the same with our soul mate at hand. Glasses in the other hand we raise them up through the month and higher on our feast day, sitting with my bracelet hand in yours.

We sincerely joined our hands while our bracelets were touching, thank you for making it for me; I continue to bring them both together nightly. I can almost smell the pies ready as they were the last morning we prepared them together, combined with the sweet apple juices already simmering in the turkey...predicting the gravy. The homemade cranberries and stuffing, the sweet potatoes baked and dumplings, enough food to keep us 'til the night falls and we bring the desserts out, bring the hot cider and chocolate out and sit out on the field all night.

So good the tastes have not left our celebration, the memories as fresh on my pallet as they were the last day we feasted with you here, to keep the inspiration the same. Each year we celebrate thanks for giving day for the month the same.

`For music you bring
and the words that match,
the handclapping for rhythm
that brought our souls back.
For the true love

that which is shown,
for the earnest compassion
our souls have grown.
Over and again you have presented
the height that could be reached,
from the time we met
you two combined,
life soared to completion.
We brought contentment
when we joined as one,
when rejoicing together
life began,
you gave it to us
with you two combined
for that...
we thank you together'

More words said on thanks for giving day about us,
the celebrations still to this day are as incredible as they
were. I am so tired from the hours we were up and from
the amount of tears poured. People came back around
that we have not seen for years, we ate and laughed and
cheered, tear up just from seeing them it reminded me of
you all night, and all day too. I wish you were here
relaxing in this mood with me, pleased, smiling because
of realized dreams, we believed so came true. Kissing
you, missing you, blissful once again with your smile,
spending the night away with you.

Bethinking you. I remembering sitting in the canoe on
the lake taking black and white photos of you and you
of me. It was autumn this particular time I recall, much
like the one this one has been. Images of you with the
apple tree in the background, and others with the

theatre...taking mine the same.

I can almost see on your lips my name, and other words said, or maybe I remember so easily the days the words come back the same. Tossing petals in the sky I love you, and miss you and will until I make it to you. The greatest part of you known was the happiness you brought, love sought that came out, your peacefulness brought hope. I hoped for you and you came out today. My dear you were waiting for me on that same stage in which I was brought to too, we wish and it comes true we all continue to believe to prosper from that. I wish you could be with me now, be for me now, leave with me when I am ready to go...just as soon as I recount the rest of living life with you and without you now too.

My birthday celebrating it again soon, the apple pie I still find too difficult to do, but I do, still light a candle in the middle like you did and told me to continue too when you are gone. My last birthday spent with you I know it well, see you lighting the middle telling me to wish well, yell it out loud for it to come true. Sharing my slice with you for good luck. My birthdays with you I probably miss the most, most likely as much as I long for preparing yours again, take you down by the gazebo again, horse-drawn carriage with the bamboo torches lighting the way, over the bridge to where the theatre is. Take me in, sing for me again, on the piano place look at me with your eyes closed again, `Merry of Your Start' that song already plays in my heart and my birth date is not even here.

One more birthday anniversary with us laughing through the day, in a hot bath, drinking champagne or

wine at night. Revealing your gift to me. It was most beautiful for you to make it for me, the painting with a collage of your songs written on it. Sheet music painted in all directions, the colors matched directly to the meaning. Sang the music of its middle, the new one written for that day, my birthday, even had the ones from birthdays passed up on it, and all the other ones written for me up to that day painted on it too.
It hangs in the piano room where it went after you gave it, and has stayed here this long. When I sat with my back to yours on the piano place, I would choose from the canvas a song just for me. On my birthday and every other day you made me feel special, but, of course extra special on the day I was born!

Everything stayed the same through the years as we aged, understood the meaning much clearer for what we were born for. Our ambition remained for what we knew was needed, wanted for as a whole. My heart full with joy to be able to write about it now, as I planned to do all along, much how you left for me your songs in the order we were given.

`Happy birthday today
 the pleasures you bring to me
I will sing to you every year
 how happy you make me
how excited I get
when this day nears,
happy day for me too
I am so in love with you
so happy you were born today
merry birthday...'

Merry birthday to me. I awoke this morning to this song awakening me inside, therefore I will play it today while I try the pie.

Eyes wide open now, I stretch outside to the snow falling, a winter paradise upon the field now that the leaves are gone. The first snowfall, looks like it is going to stay, the flakes are strong enough to stay on the grounds and the trees, waking me up for my day.

I plan to have breakfast in the piano room, while listening to you about me, while looking at the canvas imagining you first giving it to me. Sit amongst the flakes with a hot mug of cider while the pie is getting ready, I should also get the torches ready for the carriage ride.

Recorder alongside me where you sat, I feel it has gotten much warmer since the last torch you lit, I will never forget the site, of you waiting for me by the carriage that night. Every night my birthday came around, waiting for me with flowers in your hand, taking my hand, holding it for as long as we stay out that night, and through sleep too. My last birthday the most sad, happy as usual, we just knew you were going, knew that this one would be the last. We talked about it and felt the same as the last one I prepared for you, so hard to do, but I still do. I celebrate our births as if you were here, sometimes with friends near, this one spent alone. Now in the bath reading me.

Chapter five, Bon Voyage:

I set off earlier today. The sun was bright, and it is quite warm. I have everything I need to venture the oceans, to cross the seas, to get through storms and great heat...all I need I have to relax me. I am not too sure when I will be back, I'll keep the days passing weeks months years, the wind will someday guide me back. Already I enjoy my voyage afloat, big strong sturdy boat holding me up. Gaff placed between a makeshift holder of rocks, socks off feet hanging down to the water, nothing but open water for miles is all I see on this selfless insulation, catching fish, deciding which way to row.

Hmm, now I choose south, the direction the birds go when everything gets cold, now it is still quite warm as the sun has already gone down, and every star you must be able to see. Relaxing on what seems to be the middle of the sea, drifting me into what I need it.

The start of my new island adventure has begun! I hope to rest about thirty days row away from here; on an island quite similar to the one I have become accustomed to. But now I miss the open water, so I pack up and head where the waves during this season flow; stopping in thirty days or so to rest upon another peaceful place...

I did not hope but I figured it would be true, this year this day in particular to be difficult without you, eating the pie without you once again, it is proven year after year as much as I try to swallow it is hard to do. You left the recipe for me and I am glad you did, but I will never forget the tastes of you getting this day ready for me, still merry of my start. But it is unequal celebrating alone, with all the well wishes I appreciate wholeheartedly...there was still you missing.

I miss you kissing me awake singing happy birth date, you reaching over to the table and presenting breakfast to me; orange-champagne drink and everything else you knew I loved for morning eating. Eating face-to-face with thee, smiling, laughing, chatting of past birthdays spent traveling, spent right here at home. The bubbles from the champagne tickle my nose as I sit with memories flashing by me, so many to pick just one out...they all feel the same.

You call my name and for real I can hear it, you said it enough to replay it easily. You knew just where to touch me to get my shadows moving, my spine straight to you, and curled back from you. Touching me, I am old enough now for sure to know what we were doing to get us going, we knew where we were going so we went. We joined together like the harmony moving through my words written, your music written, like the petals blending in the water felt upon our bodies to raise the shivers further. You were really good at stroking your hands on me like that, while pledging to me like that of your love and how happy you are that I was born, said it was to complete you.

You completed me, I knew when I first spoke with you of your intents completely, I felt thee, you felt like me. I knew I met my soul mate when I met you, you looked like I did the same at life, eyes just as deep. We kept the same hours up through the days, or nights, had the same ideals as everyone else we knew. I am still growing. As old as I am now, there is still knowledge to be knowing, more beats to move to and songs to top off my soul to undercover things thought known.

It meant everything showing myself through you, what you inspired me to keep me creative, keeping my mind alert in production today. Deciding what else to leave. We said enough words to each other before you left to keep me and the others too, the same meanings with different words and the exact words over and over, it helps us to understand life to keep it smoothly moving forward.

It is so real, everything is as vivid as when you were present; it is winter although, it is as bright as if it was summertime...looking 'Up at the Sky'
Looking at the evening sky
I see a clear picture of thee,
that is all I imagine
the stars to be.
 When it is as bright as
it is in the dark, I look to hope to see you
I do,
I see you as often
as I want to,
as frequently as the nights permit .
When the calmness of the lake
reflects your image from the sky,
I am torn between where to focus my eyes, so it has taken me a long time to recreate this painting, the one I gave to you later in the winter.

You said it was absolutely beautiful, the tears in your eyes said it truly, you held it with open arms and told me it was absolutely beautiful, so beautiful, most

beautiful. I told you, 'I know you will be here for me
after you go, you are embedded in the fibers of my soul,
before I knew, that feeling in my heart was you before
we met, who I had to seek, meet, and greet with warmth
every morning and before sleep...throughout all day. I
wish you could have stayed, but I know you will be
here, looking up and down at me, if I look to the lake I
will see you, and if I look to the sky there you be. It will
be difficult as well for me, this painting is for you now, I
hope you leave it for me later, to remind me where you
are when I need you...'

And then we held one another and fireworks
happened through the night.
The fireworks happened. I enjoy those memories of our
visits to the cottage, the ocean beside us caused our
desires to be moving. With the fireplace lit and flowers
over the bed...a trail to the bathing room, in the tub,
glasses filled and plenty of food, we spent weekends and
full weeks there when it was our turn. When it was our
time to use it we definitely enjoyed it, sitting on the
porch in the morning looking cross at the mountains,
drinking something cold or hot depending on what
season we were there.

We spent many winters there, I have not been there
since you were here, the memories are near though, we
loved the times in the summer there, we were able to
camp outside there. In the wintertime it was too windy
there, we held each other by the fire, natural sounds
around. The crackle from the fire, your hands caressing
me, the fierceness of the wind, my hands on thee, our
sounds together. The sounds we made I hear, I feel your
hands and I am beside myself, memories come back and

I cannot help myself from recalling, from welling up in my eyes. I want to sleep sometimes because I am so much more tired than before, but my mind is awake, you know I still sometimes stay up for nights, even at the age I am.

I will never forget you up too, all night, naps through the day, waking up inspired again. Our dreams secure in us enough to keep us going, our minds flowing in the order our hearts know, souls guiding us when we were young and learning. As we were growing older before we knew it our time together was over, oh how the days past. The former days I sometimes mix up with the present, I love the memories I be keeping so close to be to be able to make so vivid, especially now with all the time in back of me.
What is left before me is what I have had all along, writing on the back flashes flashing before me now. The things ahead of me I promised you I would leave it, you vowed to keep the same word to me through your recipes and music. Your paintings and your love letters for me, I have included some of them in what I am leaving, just as you did in your book for me. I wish you could be here to read it coming together now and play inspiration for me.

Up on the bench, a master on the keys, in life itself, everything you were suppose to do you did well. Spoke well, walked well, helped us the way you knew to and loved to, said it put your spirits back in place. I agreed with you, followed you, you warmed your hands the way mine were, when we were younger, and learning, deep breathing, eyes deeply. We stretched to the morning even if the birds were gone for the winter, like this morning they are, therefore, I stretch to the stars that are out with me on the mornings that are clear. Otherwise to the smell of the snow and crisp clear breeze, the lake, the apple pancakes baked, or something of the like; just the same as if you were around. I hear your relaxing moans now freeing the throes of me, growing old with the sounds from what I remember. Concentrating on hearing you next to me in the morning and before I sleep too, anything I can do to keep you close, until I am back with you.

You come back to me in my dreams some nights, pressed snugly against mine, your hand on my hand fondling the bracelet you gave, whispering to me. Sometimes I cannot make out what it is you are saying to me, but I know it is appeasing me, pleasing me, I can tell by the way I am moving around, the way I am smiling. The way I wake up in the middle of the night, or not 'til morning, heart racing moving around and smiling the same, calling your name realizing you are not here. After all these years, still, I continue to rise up in the morning just realizing you are not here, it is difficult to bear, even if I do see you when I want. I hear you when I need to and feel you like before, all I need I know is to touch you one more time, who knows when I will see you again.

Until then, when I see you forevermore, up to the time my spirit combines with yours anew...and with our friends, I will sit around and recount what I promised around you, when I made a vow to myself to leave what we have now; to keep the same feelings round. The height of our intellect, the warmth from our glow, the knowledge of our souls combined, the life and living it with pure love. Living with you and our friends with you purling about in peace, is with us all now, somehow we came together and realized we need it the same. Want family and friends, enough food to bring them around, a place to relax, words to give them when they give us theirs. The clear air we bring is what we offer with our natural talent, our purpose for life given to us we shared.

We continue to share, after all these years we continue sitting in circles around the world, dance in circles round the world...sharing what we know. It was because our souls felt the same, cried inside to get us together to make changes in the world. Sang and wrote about the joy we would bring if we brought ourselves together, every soul we meet, no matter what the background be.

We came together long ago because we had to, we were growing further and further away from what we first knew, what we were born here to do, brought that knowledge back, which brought our souls back. Backs pressed together the way we did before, hands warm, tight hugs naturally peace came back along, in its true definition.

With its true definition being within all of us, that is what it means in itself, now that all of us have felt it, and feel it strongly enough to keep it up, now life we have one. We all have something to pass down to keep those after us at ease, pleased with who they are, where they came from, and what they know because we shared.

Our time-shared spending laughter in the snow, making angels and sitting in them drinking cider to keep warm. The sun shining as if it is summertime we always said while looking at the sky. I sit on the bench and it appears to be just the same looking up, and if I concentrate enough on the heat I can feel it through the cold. Warming me as I watch people skating on the lake. It is always pleasant coming out to the sounds of excitement on the domain, the little ones playing games together as the bigger ones circle around. I have not been on the ice in years, the last time was with you here.

Now I enjoy sitting out with our hot apple cider, baked products, stew and sandwiches, or if friends arrive early enough we sit and enjoy pancakes. No matter where we travel we have this, sharing all it is we have, I still love cooking so I make sure I do it as often as I can. Even if you are not around to help anymore, I feel you helping in spirit... that is what everyone else says too.

I am not too old to continue our, 'Kindness on Humans Path' in fact, it causes me to become more alive from deep inside each time I come out to greet, we speak with sincerity with whom we meet and continue to know. Wearing snowshoes now that the snow is high enough to need them, across the field I ventured this evening to rest me before sleep.

I have been able to sleep these past few nights, spent them dreaming about you. You spend the most peaceful moments with me, which is why it makes them so. I have felt you next to me since before we met, so it is easy to hold onto these feelings now, with me as the way you were long before we met.

Long before we got to know, but we certainly felt it,
you told me the same thing when you met me, the more
time spent with me, you said you knew I was that
feeling that enlivened your inner most substance.
Substantiating me. There was something about the way
I moved to thee, with thy, why oh why did you have to
die so soon, your body gave up on you, but I feel you the
way I felt you before.

Before the sky tonight as if it is summertime, I sit, stars
as clear as they can be, the moon in its second phase, the
lake a slight rage. There is sweet moisture in the breeze
reminding me of times former, of your sandal wood in
the wind, of catching your whispers in my heart. It is
now the start of the morning and I must now go inside,
light the fire and settle down for the evening, hopefully I
will see you tonight.

For loving me right and teaching me well, for listening
to me and hearing me true, for keeping me close and
even in spirit, for the love we made and keep on making.
For the cider and apple pie recipe...the immaculate
combinations we moaned and we sighed with. For the
moaning and sighing, the feeling of belonging, my dear
darling one I will love you for always, and eternally. I
will love you like I vowed to love you in the beginning,
it is still not the end. I will write of our love to the end
of my time, leave it all behind to teach what it was that
we were taught.

What it is that we learned is that we are all the same,
just the same, want and long for the same. We grieved
the same when we lose ones close, we all have tears
when a new spirit is born. We savor our food and cook

it homemade; we share what we have we all want it the same. Life is the same worth living it well, the best part of our life is seeing everyone smiling, truly. You are truly missed. I wish you were around for this, in body as well as mind and spirit, just so I can embrace you, hug you kiss you once again.

Just one more time I would like to come in from the snow with you, sit by the fire after a tangerine bath in the blanket I made for you, big enough for me too. I sit in it wrapped up alone. After spending the evening outside, the bath was the spot to be inside, sitting now on your side of the bed, waiting for dawn to come.

You were the one and only love for me and I was the same for you, we were enough and lasted long enough for me to live out life now alone. I have you here sitting on my spot as I am occupying yours, I want to reach out and touch you, but I know you are a mirage stopping by. I know my time is drawing to an end, you visit me so often sometimes I am not sure where I am, my imagination continues to be as creative as if it were times from before. I feel the same looking at you now even if I must close my eyes and focus as much as I can. I can reach out and take your hand and place it in mine as if before, fall asleep with your hand in mine as long as I concentrate I sleep.

It is much easier when I am sleeping for I do not have to focus at all, you hear my calls before I speak you are there as my eyes close. Not quite ready to close them forever as I am awakened in high spirits to begin the next days, more to write on the things we did and what I continue to do alone and with our friends.

Our friends are coming over this morning to get it ready for all the guests that have been skating, each morning since the lake has been solid, was the amount of folks that could be on it. Five o'clock in the morning they said they would be here, so I got up earlier to prepare myself for when they come. I am ready for when they arrive, they said we will start everything together, they always brought fresh eggs and milk over, so I have to wait anyway 'til when they get here. Not too long now! Everyone enjoys your pancake-baked recipes with apples in it, or on it; we will be making enough of them this morning. A pot of cider over the fire burning overlooking the lake, homemade bread toasted with homemade apple jam, and the ones our friends will bring made the same...sides to match the pancakes and bread.

We will have enough food to extend ourselves to luncheon time, mid-afternoon. The soup now simmering next to the cider over a fire of its own, sandwiches ready to warm next to the cider, as we get the chocolate ready for the hot chocolate. For supper time we will go to the theatre, we have been back and forth from it all day, getting ready for whose birthdays are this month. I am included this day today and all night with all the other birthdays.

Each candle on the table lit, cakes are done, we made enough bread this morning for all day and night long. Songs have been playing since I woke up this morning, the apple cheese casseroles are prepared for the oven, the chowders are slow-cooking, we made a choice of

three, salads and everything else now ready to celebrate.
`Happy birthday to all of you and to me...let us feast and
drink and stand from our seats to the beats. Thank you
for coming around, drink down and be merry of you'

Last evening and this morning bring about the same
air, celebrating the month's end with birthday cheers;
candles lit felt like you were here. As I sit near to the fire
with everyone now gone, I play your songs and sit
comfy in the blanket waiting for what to recall.

I recall you dancing, dancing for me, fire burning like
right now, in the morning or in the afternoon, and for
sure by evening you moved your way toward me. All
morning or day you worked on me, or through my
dreams, waking me up dancing towards you, your spot.
Fires burning, moving for you, we kept the house hot
this is why you are with me now. I feel you in the
blanket with me as I go back and feel what it is in my
mind. We always kept the passion flowing from what
our hearts felt, from what we know for sure; I know now
you are here with me, I know you have not left me at all.

This morning has been like most others this winter,
looking all around, the sky as bright as it can be, even
with the ground packed with snow. The branches
making music and I stretch to their movement, moving
no differently from when you were here, awakening
with peace with me.

You are still wanted in the mornings just as the sun
rises, breathing, stretching, content with life, deciding
which flowers to choose. Preparing breakfast while
getting ready for dinner, it has been so long since those

times, along aside me. A long time ago you were always beside me, across from me, at my feet, working with me, loving me. I never imagined this amount of time without thee, I am ready to go, my soul is full. I need your warmth for right now the sky is not enough for me, the blanket I made for us needs us, my flowers in the vase need yours.

I am ready to be with you like before, start where we left off before we knew you were going. My age showing yet I have so much more to write, my mind awake with my spirit and I miss you, want to see you again. I will go on writing for as long as I know I can, I am ready when you are because I miss you, would like to come back to you, am pleased with what life has given me this long. I just long to hear your songs through you, up all night and day serenading me, and me you, you know words with music to match the feeling of living life like this, so happy for so long.

We are all long lasters of love, the energy around us feels the same...like love and peace and happiness, happy with me even though I am often sad, recalling feelings had and how they continue to be with me.

Calling my name the same as before, never quite the same way, it depends on which season it is, now that it is winter your call to me feels warm, warming me through the cold. I tend to look at the sky when I think I hear you call, and then I put my ear to it and hope to hear what I think I did again. And I do, I hear you calling me out over the breeze, 'return to me please' these patterns in my days keep me alive, they wake me up to what my dreams have inspired me to all night.

I light the candles on the table and sit at the window's bay, the flawlessness of this winter day makes it easy for me to write, your music in the background is delightful to hear, fingers dancing blissfully about, sounds like spring is here.

The height of the 88
the depth of the keys
matched you,
the flight that which
you brought me to
I brought you too,
this is what you said
and what you would if sitting at the bay with me
starting to write, got us in the mood to create just from
sitting with each other, no matter where we were. I can
probably trace back in order the way we found
ourselves together, although we came together before
we realized, but once we did we stayed together. When
talking about past moments shared, we could see we
loved one another from the first image captured of us on
the same stage.

It is the first picture in the album you titled,
`Absolutely You and I' our first embrace, our eyes both
closed, chin on each other's shoulder, hands pressed on
my back on yours. It is obvious even from the side of
our faces the passion in which we felt then, the
beginning looks like our end. The last picture is the
same, same spot same embrace same tears running
down our faces. Holding one another not letting go in
the beginning and not wanting to in the end, my best
friend was you. That feeling of completeness was there
with you and still now that you are gone, it is still the

way it was before you were gone.

   With great spirits you are here. With the three of you
gone, there are three of us here, still the closest friends
getting together the days we planned. We were a close
circle of friends, we sit here now at equal space apart
from one another longing for the same. Our soul mates
off together like we are roaming about with grace,
leaving the space next to me for you and the others for
our friend's mates.

   We stand strong and toast we know to stay positive
through you all gone, we listen in the background to
your singing and recount times that made us tear up we
laughed so much. The fun in all of us through the years
is with us as we go back on memories to make more.
We can feel our hearts filling up and pouring from the
time we get together, toasting to the days ahead.
Handclapping keeping the beat, signing our names to
what we create. Eating apple _____, apple
_____and apple _____, (these recipes have
already been included) merry the afternoon away. On
the canvas we wrote together what came about as the
night fell upon us, stars bright as is the moon and our
thoughts came about on the canvas together. We made
our way over to the theater, allowing the painting to dry
where we were to keep it.

'For what life brings us
we are complete,
we toast first to
completeness here...here, here.
We are whole
from coming together,

we know
our souls could feel it,
a toast to our souls
here, here.
To the energy around here; here, here!
For our community here; here, here!
Unity; here, here!
To the peace love and happiness here; here, here!
For what we offer our life here; here, here!
To our friends around the world and those here; here,
here!
For what life brought us
and continues to bring
we toast to all
and everything here,
here, here'

The theatre will start up again tomorrow. We hung
the canvas in the lobby where people like to gather
before and after the celebrations, especially since it is
winter. We have the lighting softly around the painting,
highlighting the words through the dimness, the image
in the background seen from a different perspective. We
painted it first. In the afternoon we had the oil paints
out and took turns with the brushes, something we said
we would do yearly when we got together... a
homemade gift from us to all of our friends. It is what
we feel our souls to look like when we close our eyes to
see it, and the words it might say. Thankful for
everything it has at hand.

I am thankful for our friends. We get together now
whenever we can, we have more time to gather, but less
time left so we make the most from it. We have not

forgotten why we knew we should start to gather and held each other in the same regard from when we first met. Mature now, we all have pure heads, speaking of what first came to mind; one hundred percent we knew to put in it, to raise us to this point we now have, so glad we made it.

We all have made it, we now know to keep us up to keep all of us to the point that is needed, created what we were all seeking and so therefore we are at ease. The comfort inside is different, it is like we have been sleeping outside in nature, kept by the energy around. Walking joyfully the grounds, pleased with what is seen, keeping us of lasting quality.

The warmth keeps us year round, it is found inside and works its way out. I felt yours when you spoke, in the piano room you often wrote, in the kitchen preparing meals with me. I felt warmth exuding from you from the palms of your hands, you were open from the moment I met you. I felt your spirit's soul, which made mine smile, so happy to see you again. Your needs from the beginning you delivered through plea, I pleaded with thee to be with me, as you asked me please. From the warmth that came along with it, I was pleased, open to you, of course I would stay close to you at all times, we were meant to be alongside each other no matter how that be.

In spirit first you met me, now you meet me that same way. Spent a lifelong journey with me for as long as we needed, now I have you how I am suppose to, off with friends, as I lay next to our friends by the fire in the blanket I made for us. So comfortable next to them; it will be difficult after breakfast tomorrow when it is time for them to go, we still find it difficult letting our hugs go, even though it will not be too long before we get together again.

The morning today looks like it will be pleasant into the evening, that clearness of the in-between the seasons is here. I know it was this same time you said to me so long ago, that you wanted to introduce me to your friends and meet new ones with, celebrate with, work with. You let it be me who brought you the same, brought along gifts on no particular days, but special ones for sure. Awoke in the morning with the same expressions as before; my heart now is bleeding, not that I am alone, I have all that I need. I miss you as I recall this life we knew to live it as I continue it with friends.

Chapter six: Continuing with the Sea

I decided not to count the days, the waves know which way to take me, how long I should stay upon them. It has been beautiful for nights, the stars mark the sky with each constellation out. Anchor out; I see the brightest star is out and the color around it these nights, the orange is pale but is obvious tonight and the past nights so far. All the spring stars are out as I rest relaxing steady on the night water, dolphins swimming by me, canvas beside me marking this down. A perfect night for fishing as the gaff quickly caught for me, a light feast under the stars steadily upon the water.
Anchor raised up continuing with the flow of the water, as easy as it is I am relaxed enough to sleep each evening time without worry. With the stars bright enough to mistaken the late night with early, eager for the journey ahead, the ocean for now my bed 'til another resting spot comes around...land home?

Sitting on the porch in the pouring rain, it has been awhile since it has looked liked this, can tell spring is near, that smell is in the breeze...blowing you by me. The great time we had in the rain, I miss holding your hand and running through the puddles. Too old to do now, but the memories bring back smiles anyhow; I am always reminded of the times we shared in the rain and the warmth afterwards. In front of the fire with a hot mug of something, wrapped up, getting ready to do something, what did not matter.
As long as we were together we were productive in our thinking, brought us closer together, for when we were not together. For now that I have you differently I have

anywhere to pick me up, especially now that our friends
are gone, they will be back. We have already decided
when would be good to gather again, those dates have
not changed since we made them, so glad we can make
it every time.
I look and I find what I know the field will grow to, the
apples too, I really miss spending time under the tree
with you. With the cider too there are memories
recalled each time I sip, the sweet flavors on my lips, my
tongue, soothing my throat, warming my belly to keep
my body. I am not sure if I quite got it like you, it is
satisfying and it satiates me; none the less anyway, I
wish you were here to make it.

Under the apple tree we sat here while it blossomed,
changing right before our eyes. From the moment we
planted it, it got us excited, we knew of its potential in
inspiration for us. Blossoms showered us as if it were
snowing as the time for apples got closer, wrote music
and sang to that, wrote and painted that. Right now at
the bay, I sit here having a clear view of the tree, bevel
from me, I revel in the way you looked as I sketched you
under the tree, then added your color to thee, matched
you with the scene.

I sometimes pull the paints out and recreate what we
created and take pleasure in the clear visions I remember
doing with you. With the easel on my right I keep my
journal next to me, so I can easily switch back and forth
creation flowing from me. A similar pose for you I
sketch under the blossoms falling, with an easel to your
left, I fill your sheet music around you; it is not raining.
The sky I mixed the paint a perfect blue, got the grass
just right too from adding deep yellow to the blue, and a

darker blue with a bit of white.

   Your favorite color green so I take great care in getting
it nice, especially since our view was just that, the colors
as vibrant as they can get every spring causes me still to
be inspired. I paint me next to you under the shower,
head on your left shoulder as your brush is to the
canvas, slight smiles are our expressions, showing
peacefulness.
I am at peace. Blossoms at our feet and I capture as
many falling down as were when we were under there,
as I look outside right now. It seems like the exact time
of day we spent at the bay or on the spot painted, we
look the same, just more mature in the image I captured,
capturing you with the same amount of time past as me.

   You mean the same to me. I have not counted the
days that have past, they are of no importance to me,
with the amount of time and true love had, I have
enough to keep me. Feels like you are next to me always
your spirit is near to me, dear to me, my dearest darling
you mean the same to me as I promised you would.
From way back then to this exact point in time I keep the
words the same, things done throughout the day the
same to keep me going even if sometime I get sad.

   I get sad. This time alone brings me down sometimes
even if I have all the memories to keep me going. The
memories my mind shows me, have kept you
whispering to me all along, waking me up in my sleep to
keep me lively on our path. Feelings linger around
keeping me sound even if I start to cry about you I am
happy. Quite contented. The tears that pour bring
about a peacefulness you said would keep me, 'no need

to worry when I am gone' You said you would be close,
as close as our connection was all along, 'you have my
songs which express how I have felt about you, turn me
on, whenever you want to hear my voice, turn me on
turn me up'

I have you playing. Every day since we lived together
I heard you playing, at some point of the day and
sometimes all evening, or day. I have kept you now the
same since the day it was not too difficult to turn you on.
You hold me strong with your words always so clear to
me, you loved me the same as I love you I can hear it,
feel it strongly everyday you are played and every other
time of the day, my mind on its own remembers our
days.

Our first spring evenings watching you fire dance,
danced with you, around you, brought the shakers and
drums along and made music for you. To the beat, the
fire represents you this first night of spring, sitting at the
bay watching from a distance the flames dancing about
the field.
The first morning of spring. The birds have been back
singing for a while now, awakening in the mornings
before them since this day has gotten closer. Arising
each morning with inspiration wanting to write and
paint. It has been a long time since I have painted this
much, so much so I have left the easel out, paints and
blank canvases at hand. The bay has been great,
inspiration like it has been before, sitting here gathering
sounds and visions to bring back.

The sounds are a slight moaning of contentment heard
as we greeted the mornings together, the earliest bird

with us peeping, eager for our meal. I am looking
forward to the sunflowers' seeds floating in the vase
again, with the flowers I choose to represent us, my
flowers not that lonely anymore. Not when there is
rapture and strength need I not pick the nature of what
we chose together, what automatically came to us, I set a
similar table for us.

The peacefulness at breakfast time is with me now,
your place right of me, and sometimes across from me. I
keep your chair pulled out because I have wondered
before if you were sitting next to me, for sure now I
know, have known all along from the hints of you
around.

`Come closer,
without touching you,
touching you all over.
Turning over
and over,
rolling about the field...
the bed
up dancing on the same spots,
spinning you around to me, to you...'
ecstasy for real with you as we were touching or not at
all, you twirled me around and back and again 'til we
had to fall to peace. At ease as we lay sleep, excited
through the night, still expressing how we feel, not
waking up, taking part in all aspects of our love; excited
for the time to wake up.
Next to you I wake up, delighted sparks, smiling kissing
your smile. The first time I kissed you I kissed your
smile, the second time the same way; all throughout our
lives together when kissing we kissed each other's smile.

Up on the same rock at the fall we smiled the entire time there, as did our friends, you had a smile when I kissed you for the last time.

The last kiss. It felt as if every sweet part of you was there on your lips. You slowly caressed my thigh as I was steady on your hip. On our side we held our opposite hand together, our bracelets brushing, still kissing your smile, you take yours off and hold it for a moment, closed your eyes and talked on it the same way we did all along, said, 'my love will hold strong' And you placed it on the same wrist on me that graced yours from the time our vows were first said. I kissed your smile I knew you were leaving and you did too...you gave me what has kept us close in hand our entire lifetime together. My hand in my own. We promised to give our bracelet to the other as soon as our souls knew it was leaving, you kept it on to the last moment you could.

Remembering our last kiss. Your last breath felt on my lips, as I kissed your smile, I could not let go of kissing your smile, you smiled for me. No matter what we were doing you were always so pleased, just like me, pleased to simply be; I could not stop kissing your smile as I lay on my side. Caressing your body one last time, kissing your smile the last time, saying good-bye for now I will see you soon, be sure to come back to me now.

You are and always have been my most dear friend, my best friend, and you will be for as I have known to hold you in my body that way. Your music is the background setting, bringing me to my desired tone as I drift into creation, creating your smile on the canvas painting again. At the bay once again being drawn in by the words you sing, the memories of your lips respiring your inspiration to me the last time is expressed on this canvas.

Inspiring me, I have been since you were gone still moved by you. Like I said before anywhere I look you have left an image of you, a photograph of you for me to recreate with my brushes. To later write about what was inspired relaxes me as I smile over the creation with admiration, no matter where I relax.

I am relaxed. I have spent a lot of time this spring here at the bay, watching the field come alive, painting of what is inside me. Writing of how we caused each other mutually to feel to keep us going, I am still going on with these feelings as they come up I write them down. I paint so that at a glance I see your smile smiling for me from the last time I remember it to look like. It looks the same. I have kept that image in the forefront of my mind, you were so peaceful, so happy, especially next to me for the last time.

Kissing your smile, my lips painted slightly touching yours, accepting your energy, smiling for you. Hanging to dry, in the room I will keep it I take it to dry, so beautiful there I cry myself to sleep.
I stir just before the new day begins; my dream had us in the kitchen preparing food, apple _____,
_____, and _____ too (I will leave these recipes for you) I am in the mood to begin to prepare for our friends will be here tomorrow evening. The first day of summer is here and we promised certain days to get

together for sure, this one being one. My dream made it easy for what to decide to cook; now I am making the homemade bread to go with the spread of our combinations combined.

The flowers I will gather just before they arrive and display them in every room we will be in, looks like it is going to be raining, so most of our time will have to be inside. Not that we will mind, from any spot in any room is inspiration from its view, from how we speak too. We have always put our heart in our food, still as satisfying as it in the past was, enough to cause us to hum as we eat.
The peacefulness we kept we keep, as the three of us sit together, we plan tomorrow to go to the cottage one last time together before we pass it down...when there were just three of us left to dedicate.

We keep everything we need there, the pantry and freezer stocked, we each fill a small basket up of things we want to take. I bring the paints. We plan to leave something created together for the new guests, something similar to what was left for us. The same size painting to add to the same wall. I have also brought sweet grass and candles along and your music recorded for this day, I have not forgotten to bring.

The boat-ride there gave us time to think about what to put on the canvas, not that we did any particular planning, we always set the canvas up and went naturally from there. But we were not sure where to start, we had many things we wanted to paint and say. The painting that was left for us is divided evenly to express both things, so we have decided to do the same.

   We placed the blank canvas next to the one completed and extended the image as it seems to be intended, on the right wrote what our friendship means, and what this cottage has meant, and how we hope the same for them and meant it. The colors blend in perfectly, we hang the paintings together as close as we can...the words of friendship begin on the right.
I will have to recall them later.

   `I want to thank the two of you here this evening celebrating what friendship is all about, to make life work out...here, here. For so many years the toasts made real, or life made the toasts for real!...here, here. Our soul mates are in spirit here, our circle remains the same here, content with life made here, we toast to the memories made here... here... here'

   We said good-bye the next morning to the cottage, rode backwards in the boat on the way home until it was out of view. Back home now in a mood that makes me smile, our friends will be back around before fall to celebrate the day we vowed, that date is coming on soon.

   At the falls, not on the rocks but on the grass we sit with a picnic, including wine, dried homemade bread and apple cheese, fruit slices; a tradition summer feast. We spent much of our time writing and painting, I shared words I always wrote this day on the same paper we consistently have.

I shared the book of words you wrote for me and bounded in yearly order, played music to match the arrangement too and we went back and sat out under the tree one last time together as three.

Another friend has gone. After the ceremony was held the two of us went in our room named Sanctum Ness, created to visit after the waterfall for sure. We need it now. Looking through the windows at the spectacular view, the two of us sit static stature for now, listening to music in the background you left to bring up these times. At such a time as now it is difficult not crying, consoling one another by remembering the times to keep our spirits up.

Our circle is almost complete. With each passing I know my time too is coming, still relaxed to that, still anxious to join with you whenever I am suppose to. Sometimes I still want to go, but the memories wake me up revived, even if our circle has changed, we sit as close together as we in the past have, besides we know the four of you are.

Looking at the stars so bright the moon, we went down under the tree for a clearer view. Sparked the fire, drank down the spiced cider, and sat supporting one another as we gazed at the depth of the atmosphere. Yearning to be nearer, but content with writing down here, even if we are down down here we know we will be there with you soon. We must continue to turn to each other and use the memories we made especially for this time, but more to keep our entire life pleasant.

Life was pleasantly peaceful, perfectly paced, with pied pen friends we lived our life great, walked as many

places as we could to gather knowledge for our spirit.
Our souls already knew. Our journey joined with
people wherever we went, all the simple pleasures
eagerly shared to bring peace and relaxation through the
days to bring about a carefree repose.

`For many years
we have visited this locus,
passed down to us
to focus on each other.
As young lovers we grew
with the energy of our friends,
coming together in these very rooms
we now give to you.
Keep your union strong,
heal spiritually pain,
sit by the fire enjoying cider
in the same blanket made fore you,
now for you,
sit close enough always
keep your words dear to each other,
in every weather play
rejoice every morning the day
and evening ahead,
get together with your friends
for sure all anniversaries,
and to greet the changed seasons...
come back around
be sure to come to gather.
To the memories to continue here; here, here!

Our friendship words written on the canvas next to
the painting of all of us we left for new visitors. All
hands connected. I painted you above me, our friends

did the same of their mates. I brushed our right hand against the first painting hanging; to two spirits here before...our left connects with our friends in the middle, and theirs with our friends on the end, one has their left hand raised to the side, the other to the sky...for the new painting to begin.
Generations connecting friends, `GENERATIONS CONNECTING FRIENDS' is its proper title, what we kept in mind when we were planning it on the boat ride, an easy title to live by. Our predecessors left us similar knowledge for us to develop from them, recipes, music, instruments, words with wisdom, wisdom through song.

It was not too long before we caught on, danced to our heart's beat, to the one our forbearers stepped, to develop the land well. Traditional ways of making food kept our bellies full, the positive thinking kept our bodies young to our old soul. With the knowledge learned we taught, we listened, we heard the calls well, living well amongst one another.

I sit at the window's bay where I am most comfortable these days, looking out the window across the lake.

Act two, scene two.
Spotlight on Serwa, young Serwa walks to the piano music and rests in the spotlight...Serwa begins, young Serwa hears.

Take my hand young Serwa and walk with me, let us start a new journey together, you and me. You a noble girl, I know my name means the same, I come from where you come from, I am no different from you.

Get on my back you have walked enough.
This road we travel on offers much hope, I hope you see
it, push through the days as difficult as they may
sometime seem, take my hand or get on my back
whenever you need. We are not alone, we have so many
things yet to achieve, to know, our souls now together
Young Serwa yet to be woman, keep your back strong,
for others who need it, my gracious young Serwa you
are needed.

Spotlight dims and lights on Chunna, and young
Chunna walking to the piano music resting next to
Chunna...she squats down.
No, no my dear Chunna stand strong next to me, rest
your back against mine and hold both my hands. You
are worthy, a beautiful girl, no need to bend down to
hide away. Use my back to lean to stand, hear my
words you have a friend of the same name. I come from
where you came from and now together we stand. Let
me see your eyes so deep you matter little girl, you are
of importance to our world I hope you know it, I will
always tell you that and hug you when you need. Keep
your back pressed to mine, I will help you to succeed.

Spotlight fades and focuses on Kimeri and young
Kimeri making her way over to the spotlight to music.
Do not be afraid, young Kimeri, I am Kimeri too, your
past is my past too. Yes I know, please don't cry, there is
hope, these tears will soon come only from joy, I am
sure. I am old enough to know how to help you, from
what I went through; let us walk together from now on.
I will teach you the songs of my heart that come from
my soul to lift you up, come here let me carry you now,
do not cry. You are a girl to become a woman ALIVE!

Seen in your face, all over your face, Kimeri, almost woman, so glad you were born.

Spotlight dims and shines on Latoya and young Latoya dancing to each other.
Let me meet you half way young praised one, help you find your way. Your grandparents were right in raising you that way, saying those great things, I heard them too. It will always matter the name given to you little girl, use it to bring you up, no matter who is around. I am here. With the same name I kept the meaning in the forefront of my head, to keep me strong, back strong, legs strong, no one will bring you down. My hand is hot, feel that spot, connect your energy to me of the same name, same sex that matters here young Latoya, please do not ever forget it.

Spotlight switches to Wuti standing on the stage with her arms open, young Wuti dancing over to the piano music still the same tone, varied tempos.
My young brilliant Wuti, how honored I am to have the same name, to be woman, to hold the life of the world in hand. That is how important it is to be a girl to grow to that, to pass on the good things our elders taught. Get on my back I will teach you too, walk through the streets with you, to make sure you stay strong. It will not take long young one, once you believe in there, right in the deepest part of you, to what got you to this point. Remember your name our elders named us that to keep us going to woman, Woman, WOMAN!

The spotlight goes to young Eileen dancing across the stage on an angle, she bows to Eileen.
So wonderful to meet you too Eileen, I am Eileen too,

here to guide you with what I know and with what I learn along the way, to able and nurture your soul. You know you are not alone, is not a question but, rather a statement, something you need to believe. Look around anywhere to see just what you have, look in the mirror, you are what you need, your name in agreement to the importance of you, soon to be woman, I am one now. So proud, stand strong next to me and take my hand, you important little one, your journey has begun and I will walk it with you, stand next to you strong to hold you up when you need. Oh young Eileen, I am so happy to have met me.

All woman lit up, in whatever order they want to the piano music...

I AM WOMAN
there is power in my name,
I AM WOMAN, A WOMAN
like you,
LITTLE WOMAN
growing into A WOMAN.
I AM WOMAN, I AM WOMAN
there is beauty in saying it,
LITTLE WOMAN, almost WOMAN
you best be believing it!
WOMAN, I am listening
I take your hand I feel it,
I AM WOMAN LITTLE WOMAN
becoming more powerful.
Taking a stand,
standing strong,
firm hands held,
wrongs healed up,

raised us up,
believing in WOMAN,
lifts us up...
WOMAN, (clap) LITTLE WOMAN, (clap) WOMAN,
(clap) LITTLE WOMAN, (clap) WOMAN, (clap) LITTLE
WOMAN, (clap) WOMAN, (clap) LITTLE WOMAN,
(clap) WOMAN, (clap) LITTLE WOMAN, (clap)
WOMAN, (clap) LITTLE WOMAN, (clap)

And they kept clapping, the celebrations after the
show kept us to the beat, clapped the night away with
the friends kept, ones met, promises made to keep. The
beats here keep us to our feet, to steady us on the streets,
towards everyone we meet we greet in high spirits, take
them in. A friend to everyone we meet, 'keep us the
same, keep this ambition forever on our land, hold
hands, take stands, celebrate you with the world as often
as you can here, toast again, make your beginning be
much like the end, steady the middle too, study lots too.
My friends here tonight and in spirit too, this night has
come to an end, I welcome you back again whenever
you can come here'

The theatre was always warm, as I look over at it I can
hear the words as clear as when they were said,
forgotten not about the faces of all who were there, who
came back all the time and brought new friends around.
The energy of past times is still there now, all around it,
on the lake and in the field. I sit under the apple tree in
spirit writing our life and our time shining as we
roamed the earth bare foot.

Life before you, with you and after you was perfect;
precisely our hearts followed the destination of souls,

our souls so close together now. I know that I have grown to the height of what was desired, so tired...I end the pages and sign initials to it, I hope you add yours, so this life I lived so gracefully will gracefully brush yours. ALM

Quote Book...
...By us each day, the same one for one week for our
time.

Week 1:
One hundred percent of positive ness will raise us to the point of successful ness, in reaching our level of human kindness.

Week 2:
Accept the knowledge your soul acquires through the day.

Week 3:
Heal pain spiritually.

Week 4:
Sing over and over and over and over.

Week 5:
Enjoy eater, we all know the reason.

Week 6:
Undercover things not yet known, or believed.

Week 7:
Exude your energy positively.

Week 8:
Celebrate your birthday; be merry of your start.

Week 9:

Welcome the knowledge of combined security.

Week 10:
Open up completely spiritually.

Week 11:
Stay on the Kindness of Humans path.

Week 12:
Smile.

Week 13:
Tend to the land and plant seeds.

Week 14:
Enjoy the sun when it is out, you don't know when the cloud will roll in.

Week 15:
Give tight hugs; they put your spirits back in place.

Week 16:
Call in pleasant points in time always.

Week 17:
Forget not about the first thing you wanted to become.

Week 18:
Eat breakfast to strengthen your days, lunch to extend
your breakfast, and supper to hold you over until
breakfast.

Week 19:
Breathe in the freshness of the new day and stretch.

Week 20:
Laugh often until your cheeks hurt.

Week 21:
Keep a few good friends to celebrate with, and party
with the world.

Week 22:
Enjoy the rain; you never know when the sun will be
back.

Week 23:
Combine the knowledge we all believe.

Week 24:
Eat snacks in between throughout the days.